The Arabian Nights

To Andrew, who loves good stories,
and to my grandma Hanneh who showed
me their beauty — W . T.

To my love, Flavio, and Noah: "beautiful as the moon when it's full."
To Mathis the star dreamer.
And with special thanks to Marlena Torzecka — C. H.

Barefoot Books, 2067 Massachusetts Ave, Cambridge, MA 02140

First published in the United States of America in 2010 by Barefoot Books, Inc
This paperback edition first published in 2011

Graphic design by Penny Lamprell, Lymington, UK
Color separation by Grafiscan, Verona, Italy
Printed in China on 100% acid-free paper by Printplus, Ltd
This book was typeset in Lynton BQ, Youngblood and Pabst Oldstyle
The illustrations were prepared in acrylics

ISBN 978-1-84686-568-8

Library of Congress Cataloging-in-Publication Data for
the hardcover edition is available under LCCN 2008028159

3 5 7 9 8 6 4

The Arabian Nights

Written by Wafa' Tarnowska
Illustrated by Carole Hénaff

Barefoot Books
step inside a story

Contents

Introduction

The Arabian Nights, or "The Thousand and One Nights," is a collection of fables, fairy tales, adventure stories and historical anecdotes from across India, Persia and the Arab world. The stories were collected over several centuries by storytellers, authors, translators and scholars. The oldest Arabic manuscript (a few handwritten pages discovered in 1948) comes from Syria and dates back to the early 800s. The stories are also mentioned in Ibn Al-Nadim's *Fihrist* ("Catalogue of Books") in Baghdad in 938 AD. A fourteenth-century Syrian manuscript, now in the Bibliothèque Nationale in Paris, contains some three hundred tales.

Their roots may reach back for many centuries, yet the stories in *The Arabian Nights* continue to captivate. The beauty of these tales lies in the way they weave the extraordinary and the supernatural into everyday life. Ordinary men and women meet demons and genies, princes and princesses, ghouls and magicians. Kings and queens disguise themselves as ordinary people to meet their subjects and learn to become better rulers.

And through simple storytelling, Shahrazade, a beautiful and clever woman, changes an angry and violent man, Shahriyar, into a patient, generous and kindhearted husband and father.

The Arabian Nights has become part of the world's cultural heritage. The tales have left their mark on music, art and common speech. The expressions "open sesame" and "genie," as well as images of flying carpets and magic lamps, are now widely used in films, television and children's books.

When I was a girl growing up in Lebanon, my grandmother Hanneh had only to say, "Kaan ya maa kaan" in Arabic, or "Once there was, and there was not…" for all the children to gather around to hear her retell a story from *The Arabian Nights*. Many of the stories she told had courageous heroines and princesses who helped their men in time of need. Hanneh had much in common with these heroines: the daughter of a village sheikh, she left her father's house as a bride decked with gold jewelry, sold every one of her bracelets and necklaces to educate her children, then used the rest of her dowry to dig a well in the house so that the family would have running water. I dedicate this book to her memory.

Wafa' Tarnowska

Shahriyar Meets Shahrazade

Long ago, when tales traveled along the Silk Road from China to Persia, there lived two Persian kings. They were brothers, and each was handsome, brave and loving. One brother ruled from the city of Ctesiphon in the west and the other from Samarkand in the east, so neither saw the sun set at the same time as the other.

The elder brother was called Shahriyar. The younger brother was called Shahzaman. Both brothers had married for love, not for money or status, and both were blissfully happy with their wives. They were also kept extremely busy year after year dealing with affairs of state.

However, not everything went well with the brothers' marriages. A time came when both of their wives betrayed them. Shahzaman was so saddened by this that he became a hermit and vowed never to come close to a woman again.

As for Shahriyar, he was convinced that all women were treacherous. However, he also missed their laughter and their warmth, their embraces and their jokes, their wit and their grace. What should he do? Instead of seeking someone whom he could grow to trust and love over time, he came up with the dreadful notion of marrying a new bride every day, spending the evening and night with her and in the morning having her put to death.

A month passed, during which time Shahriyar had already married thirty women and put each one of them to death. He had wedded the daughters of princes and merchants, officers and commoners — each of them just for one night. In the morning each young woman was beheaded.

A whole year passed and still no one could stop Shahriyar's madness. The task of finding a new bride each night fell to his vizier. The vizier hated this distasteful task, but he knew he had no choice. He also knew that one day one of his daughters would have to be presented to his cruel master. He was dreading that day because he had not one, but two lovely daughters. The elder was Shahrazade and the younger Duniazad.

Both daughters were as clever as they were beautiful, but of the many talents they each possessed, the most notable was Shahrazade's gift for telling stories. She loved telling them, reading them, collecting them and translating them, for she could speak several languages.

Her mind was like a treasure trove and she was full of invention too, making each story more elaborate than the next.

One day Shahrazade suggested: "Let me marry the shah!"

"Are you crazy?" the vizier exclaimed. "Who in their right mind would choose to marry him, knowing what lies in store?"

"I have no intention of dying," Shahrazade replied. "Someone must put an end to this madness and I believe I can do it."

"I will not let you endanger your life," concluded the vizier. For many weeks, he would not let his elder daughter raise the subject again. In the meantime, the city of Ctesiphon was in continuous mourning. Young women were getting scarce and the army was becoming ruthless in its search for suitable brides. The vizier felt increasing pressure to lead by example. He could hear the courtiers whispering during council meetings about how their daughters were being led to the slaughter while the vizier's were spared.

Finally, the vizier decided to let Shahrazade have her way. He and his wife wept all day as their beloved daughter was dressed for the wedding. Even Shahriyar felt a tinge of remorse at marrying the child of his trusted vizier, so he was unusually kind to her. Hence he did not say no when she asked if her younger sister Duniazad could join them at the end of the evening so that she could tell her a story before going to bed.

"But there is a condition," he said. "I must be free to listen too. What kind of story will it be?"

"The kind of story that entertains children and adults, kings and queens, the rich and the poor, the kind of story your grandmother told you when you were a boy," Shahrazade answered sweetly.

When Duniazad entered the royal bedchamber, she bowed to Shahriyar, kissed her sister Shahrazade and asked her in a low, sad voice: "Shahrazade, as this is your last night with us on this earth, can you please tell me one of your best stories so that I may remember you forever?"

Duniazad settled at her sister's feet while Shahriyar stretched on his couch, put his arms behind his head and felt himself relaxing for the first time in a year. "Maybe this bride will prove different from all the others," he thought to himself as Shahrazade started talking.

Aladdin and the Lamp

*O*nce upon a time in a faraway land lived a mischievous lad called Aladdin. Aladdin and his mother only had each other for support, for Aladdin's father, Mustafa the tailor, had died when his son was just a child.

Aladdin's poor mother toiled day and night to feed herself and her son, mending clothes and spinning cotton. She barely earned enough to put one meal a day on the table. Aladdin was easily old enough to help her, but he was lazy. He never did a stroke of work, preferring to roam the streets, playing pranks with other good-for-nothing youths.

Now one day, a tall, dark stranger came to the city where Aladdin lived. This man was an evil magician, well practiced in the dark arts. During his long years of training he had learned of a lamp, a lamp so powerful that its owner's every wish would instantly be granted. Of course, there was nothing the magician wanted more than to have this lamp, so he had studied long and hard in his attempts to locate it. He now knew where it was hidden — and he also knew that to lay his hands on it he would need the help of a small, agile assistant. So he was on the lookout for a youth who was quick and bright and who would do anything for a bit of cash.

The magician bided his time, loitering in the shadows of the souk and watching all the comings and goings. It did not take him long to notice Aladdin. One morning, the magician stopped a young lad, pressed a silver coin into his palm and, still gripping the boy's hand, murmured: "That youth over there, what can you tell me about him?"

"Oh! Don't you recognize him?" the boy asked. "That's Aladdin, the son of Mustafa the tailor, who died a few years ago. I thought everyone knew him!"

Now the magician had the information he needed. Later that day, he saw Aladdin sitting by himself. He sidled up and asked, "Are you the son of Mustafa the tailor?"

"Yes, sir," answered Aladdin, "but my dear father has been dead for a while."

"Ah, no!" cried the stranger, and he took the boy in his arms and started sobbing. "I am your uncle, your father's brother, and I have not seen him for many years, for I make my living as a merchant and I have been traveling in faraway lands."

Then he pulled two gold coins from the pocket of his silk jellabiya and pressed them into Aladdin's palm, saying: "Go and tell your mother to prepare dinner." Then he suddenly vanished.

Aladdin was reeling with shock but he ran quickly home, shouting: "Mother, mother, my uncle is back and he wants to meet you. He has given me a gold coin — can you please prepare something good for dinner?" (Aladdin, who never missed a trick, had decided to keep the second gold coin for himself.)

17

"Uncle? What uncle?" demanded his mother. "Your father never told me about a brother."

"But this man knows my father's name and his trade and he is eager to meet you," said Aladdin. "Besides, he is rich. Can you please, please, please prepare a meal for him?"

"Well, why not?" said Aladdin's mother as she stared at the shining gold coin.

That evening, the tall, dark stranger sat with his "nephew" and his "brother's wife" to enjoy a delicious meal of rice, meat and pistachio nuts, washed down with sweet pomegranate juice, followed by yogurt, dates and fragrant honey.

"So," he asked Aladdin's mother, "what future have you planned for this fine young man?"

"Well," she sighed, "your nephew likes to spend his days roaming the streets with his friends. His poor father tried everything to make him learn his trade, but he refused. Mustafa died brokenhearted, peace be with his soul, and to be honest I don't know what to do."

"I understand," said the so-called uncle, and he turned to Aladdin. "How would you feel about my setting you up in a shop selling silk and cotton fabrics? Rich men and women will flock to your door. You should make a decent living."

"I should like that very much," said Aladdin, full of excitement.

"Very well," said the magician. "Tomorrow is Friday, a day of prayer and rest. Wear this new jellabiya and I shall take you to visit some prospective clients."

The next day, the magician led Aladdin to the district where rich people had their country retreats. The two of them strolled from garden to garden, and the magician told Aladdin all about the different stages involved in making the exquisite clothes that the rich families were wearing. Aladdin was so excited, he did not notice that the magician was leading him deeper and deeper into the countryside.

In the afternoon, they stopped to share some dates, fruit and cakes and rest their feet. "Isn't it time we went back?" asked Aladdin. He didn't know where he was, and he began to feel frightened.

"No, no, no — you must wait until you have seen the most wonderful garden of all," replied the magician. He sprang to his feet and strode off. Aladdin put aside his fears and hurried after him.

They walked and walked until at last they came to a narrow valley between two high mountains. Here, the magician stopped and ordered Aladdin to gather wood for a fire. When the fire was lit, he threw in some incense and pronounced some powerful magic words.

At this, a great cloud of smoke arose and the earth trembled. Aladdin trembled too! When the smoke had subsided, the magician pointed to a heavy stone slab with a ring in its center. "Now, nephew," he said in a stern voice, "Do exactly what I say and you will be handsomely rewarded. Disobey me and you will dearly regret it."

"Yes, uncle," replied Aladdin in a small, shaky voice.

"You alone shall lift this slab of stone. Beneath it there is a narrow passage leading to three halls. Walk through each hall in turn without looking right or left. Do not even touch the walls. At the end of all three halls you will find a garden with the most marvelous fruit growing in it. Don't touch any of the fruit. Walk directly across the garden until you reach a terrace. There, you will see an alcove and in the alcove a small brass lamp shining in the dark."

"I don't know if I can even lift this stone slab," said Aladdin, regretting ever having come on this journey.

"Don't interrupt me!" growled the magician. "You will do as you're told. Take the lamp from the alcove in the wall and put the flame out. Empty the oil from it, put it in the pocket of your jellabiya and bring it straight back to me. You will be handsomely rewarded."

"What if…what if something terrible happens to me?" asked Aladdin, his knees knocking.

"Take this ring and put it on your finger," said the magician. "It will help you if you are in danger." With this, he slid a ring off his little finger and gave it to Aladdin.

"Hurry now!" he ordered. "It's getting dark."

Aladdin put the magician's ring on his middle finger and pulled at the ring in the center of the stone. To his surprise, he could lift it quite easily. Before him, as the magician had said, was a narrow passage with steps leading into a black hole. Aladdin took a deep breath and went down. After a while, he could see light ahead of him. The steps came to an end and he reached the first of the three halls. He hurried across each of them in turn, as instructed, without touching the walls. Finally, he arrived at the garden with the marvelous fruit trees. By now, he was starting to feel curious.

"I will taste some on my way back," he thought to himself.

At the end of the garden Aladdin could see a brass lamp glowing softly in an alcove. It looked utterly ordinary. "Why all this fuss about a boring brass lamp?" he thought.

From far away, he could hear his companion calling: "Have you found it? Have you found the lamp? Hurry! It is getting dark out here. Hurry back at once!" But Aladdin was not good at obeying orders. As instructed, he put out the flame and emptied the lamp of its oil before tucking it into the pocket of his jellabiya. But he dawdled on his way back, stopping to look at the fruit growing on trees and other plants.

He had been hoping to eat some, but close up they looked hard and shiny, not like any fruit he had ever seen.

"These are not real fruits, they are colored stones!" he thought. He had never seen a precious stone in his life, but he was right. The fruits of that magic garden were all gemstones: the figs were sapphires, the strawberries rubies, the pears topazes, the cherries garnets and the grapes amethysts.

"I'd better take some to my mother," he thought. "She could probably sew them on to some of the dresses she sells." So he filled his pockets with the precious fruits. He also stuffed his wraparound silk belt with silver plates and goblets from the treasure chests.

"Bring that lamp up here, right now!" shouted the magician. Then he lost his temper. "This boy needs to learn to obey orders," he thought. So he threw some grains of incense onto the burning embers. The ground shook and the stone slab rolled back into place.

Aladdin heard the rumbling above his head and the stone closing the entrance to the cave. He was trapped! He felt weak with fear. "I'll run back to the garden to see if I can get out from the other side," he thought. But the door at the far side of the three halls had also magically closed. Aladdin sat on the steps underneath the great slab of stone and started sobbing.

"Allah the Great, what is to become of me?" he cried, wringing his hands. As he did so, he rubbed the ring that the magician had given him.

In an instant, a huge genie rose out of nowhere, bowed in front of him and said: "Shabbey, Labbey, your slave is here to obey! I am the genie of the ring, ask of me anything."

Aladdin fell back in astonishment then, pulling himself together, he cried: "Please get me out of here!" In a flash, he was transported out of the cave and found himself standing beside the remains of the fire.

The magician was nowhere to be seen. Aladdin turned to thank his rescuer but the genie had disappeared. "Allah be praised!" he said aloud before setting off back to the city. When he reached home he collapsed on to his bed and immediately fell asleep.

As she watched him, his mother noticed a dingy brass lamp that had rolled out of the pocket of his jellabiya.

"Why don't I clean this old dirty lamp and sell it at the souk?" she said to herself. The moment she touched it, a huge cloud of smoke rose out of the lamp and a genie appeared before her and said in a deep, rumbling voice: "Shabbey, Labbey, your slave is here to obey! I am the genie of the lamp, your wish is my command!"

Aladdin's mother fainted right away. But Aladdin woke

up at once, grabbed the lamp and ordered: "Bring us something delicious to eat."

In an instant the genie produced two large silver platters filled with perfumed rice, tender roast lamb, a jug of delicious orange juice and two glistening silver goblets.

"Your wish is my command, master," said the genie. "Do you need anything more?"

"Thank you," said Aladdin. "You may go back to the lamp."

"How can such a huge fellow fit into such a small lamp?" his mother asked when the genie had gone.

"The space inside it must be of a different dimension from ours," said Aladdin.

After they had finished eating, Aladdin's mother suggested they sell one of the silver platters. Over the next couple of months, Aladdin sold all of the silver platters and goblets, including those he had smuggled back from the cave.

With each visit to the souk, he learned more about the value of gold, silver and precious stones. He now understood that the colored stones he had brought in his pockets from the cave were emer-alds, rubies, sapphires and diamonds. So he hid them in a strong metal casket.

Over the next couple of years, Aladdin became quite rich, thanks to the genie of the lamp and his own skills as a merchant. He bought himself a nicer house and furnished it well. His mother was able to stop work and instead spent her time visiting friends.

One day, as he was walking in the souk, Aladdin heard the sultan's heralds shouting to the crowd: "Make way, make way, lower your eyes: Princess Badr el Boudour, Moon of Moons and daughter of our beloved sultan, is passing here on her way to the hammam. If any man should dare to steal a look at the princess, he will regret the day he was born. Make way, make way, lower your eyes, lower your eyes!"

Aladdin, who never took any notice of orders, hid behind a big wooden door, determined to steal a look at the princess. And he was not disappointed. For as the convoy passed by, he peeped out and saw that Badr el Boudour herself was peering through the curtains of her palanquin. She caught Aladdin's gaze and smiled back, her green eyes glittering with laughter. Aladdin was smitten.

"Mother," he announced when he returned home, "I have fallen in love with Princess Badr el Boudour and I intend to marry her."

"But my son," she cried, "this is pure folly! No son of a tailor, no matter how rich, can marry a princess. This is an impossible dream. It is time you found yourself a wife, though. In the morning, I shall go and ask my friends if they know of a more suitable bride for you."

Aladdin's mother proposed the butcher's daughter, the baker's daughter, even the goldsmith's daughter. But Aladdin was as stubborn as a mule at the edge of a cliff.

"The only woman I shall ever marry is Badr el Boudour," said Aladdin. And he locked himself in his room and refused to eat. "Mother, you need to find a way!" he cried. "Do something or I shall die!"

So Aladdin's mother summoned all of her courage. The next day, she went to the sultan's majlis, taking as a present some of the precious stones, carefully wrapped in a silk cloth. She sat all day in the sultan's court, waiting for her turn to be heard. But she was too modest

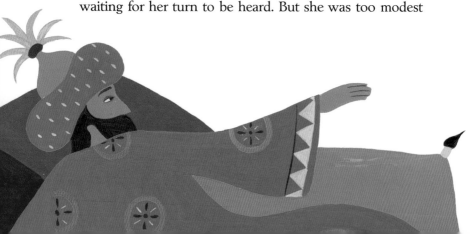

to assert herself and step forward, so her turn did not come
— neither that day, nor the day after, nor the day after that.

After several days, the sultan nudged his grand vizier and
said: "I have been noticing this woman dressed in black and
clutching a bundle of silk. She has come every day for six
days. Bring her over here so I might hear her plea."

Aladdin's mother was shaking from head to foot. She
threw herself at the sultan's feet. Then she raised her head
and said: "Sire, I am not even worthy of shining your sandals,
but my son Aladdin, son of Mustafa the tailor, has earned
great riches. Some weeks ago, he glanced at your precious
Moon of Moons, your daughter Badr el Boudour. Since that
day, he has not eaten a crumb nor drunk a drop and he has
begged me to bring you this gift in exchange for her hand."

The sultan laughed loudly at the woman's boldness, but
curiosity was nagging at him like an annoying fly. So he told
her: "I hope for your sake that this gift is worthy of the beauty

and the rank of my darling Badr el Boudour, whom your son should never have seen in the first place!"

But the moment the sultan unwrapped the silken bundle, the precious stones shone with a radiance that took his breath away. "These jewels are indeed worthy of my little princess," he murmured. Then, turning to his vizier, he said: "What do you think of this woman's demand, grand vizier?"

The grand vizier, whose honeyed tongue had enabled him to keep his post for many years, said as he examined the stones: "They are indeed worthy of our beloved princess, sire. But she is not yet seventeen. Shouldn't you make her suitor wait for at least three months until she has finished preparing her trousseau?"

"You are quite right!" said the sultan. "Tell this woman to return in three months."

What the sultan did not know is that the grand vizier wanted his son to marry the princess and needed some time to bring the sultan around to this idea.

Aladdin's mother hurried back to her son to tell him the good news. Filled with joy, he immediately started dreaming of the palace he would build for his princess with the help of the genie of the lamp.

Two months passed, with Aladdin eagerly awaiting the day when he could claim Badr el Boudour as his bride. Then one afternoon, as Aladdin's mother was buying some silk in the souk, the merchant asked: "Are you making something for the wedding feast of our princess and the son of the grand vizier?"

"The princess's wedding feast?" echoed the mother. "I must tell my son at once."

But it was too late, the princess was to be married that evening. "I cannot believe the sultan has not kept his word!" cried Aladdin indignantly. "I must stop this marriage at once!"

"My son, sometimes the wind blows the wrong way and the ship has to take a different course. Maybe you should just give up this foolish dream."

"I won't give up this dream, mother — never," said Aladdin.

At the end of the wedding feast, knowing the bride and groom would have retired to their bedchamber, Aladdin rubbed the magic lamp. "Bring the princess, her husband and their bed right here into this house," he ordered the genie.

In an instant the wedding bed covered with rose petals landed in front of Aladdin with the princess and her groom sitting bolt upright, both looking terrified.

"Take the groom seven miles outside the city's gates and leave him there," said Aladdin to the genie. The genie obeyed, and the poor groom spent all night walking back to the palace.

"My beloved," said Aladdin, kissing the princess's hands, "don't be frightened, just listen to my story. Your father promised me your hand, for two months ago I gave him the most beautiful gemstones in the world. A promise is a promise. I am only doing this to win you back. Trust me."

The princess wept at first but as she listened to Aladdin and looked more closely at him, she recognized the handsome young man she had seen in the souk. "What shall we do?" she asked, for she knew she was in love with him and had no interest in sharing her life with the son of the grand vizier.

"Don't worry about a thing," said Aladdin. "For the time being, you must go back to your father's palace, but I shall see to it that we are brought together."

The next morning, anyone who was out on the streets at sunrise would have been astonished to see a flying bed with a frightened princess on it speeding across the sky toward the palace. That same morning, the sultan and his wife woke up late and went straight to the princess's bedchamber.

"So, did you spend a happy night, my darling?" asked the sultan.

"No, I did not!" the princess retorted, and just as she had finished speaking the disheveled groom walked in, with muddy feet and a face like a thunder cloud.

"Where have you been, my son?" enquired the sultan.

"Oh, just out for a little walk," lied the young man.

For five nights in a row, the genie spirited the princess and her groom away

33

from the palace. And for five nights in a row, the poor groom was left miles outside the city and had to walk for hours to get back. On the sixth day, he requested a private audience with the sultan.

"I am deeply sorry, your majesty, but I cannot remain as your daughter's husband," he said to the sultan. "This marriage is already proving much too hard."

The sultan was furious with the young man and immediately banished him, along with the grand vizier. "You have both shamed me, and brought shame on my innocent daughter! This must be a lesson from Allah, blessed be His name. I should have kept my promise to the tailor's son. Guards, fetch me Aladdin at once!"

The moment Aladdin arrived at the palace, the sultan said: "My daughter is yours, my son. You are far more worthy of her than the son of the grand vizier!"

"I am greatly honored, your majesty," Aladdin replied. "For as long as I draw breath, your daughter will be the queen of my heart." Then, pointing to a window in the audience chamber, he said: "And this, sire, is where she will live."

Following Aladdin's finger, the sultan caught sight of the most magnificent palace he had ever seen. The lamp had worked its magic: the domes of the palace were of red and its windows — ninety-nine in total — were encrusted with crystals. The walls were of white stones, each carved by hand. The floors were of white marble and the pillars of jasper and agate. The furniture was of ornately carved sandalwood, draped with fine brocades. Every detail was exquisite.

"Allah is great," said the sultan, embracing his new son-in-law.

The wedding feast was spectacular. Aladdin won the hearts of the people that night and before long everyone forgot about his bad behavior as a youth. But far away in the depths of Africa, word reached the magician about the marvelous palace. "I thought the young scoundrel was dead," he said to himself. "He must have escaped from that cave and discovered the magic of the lamp, for no human could have built that palace. I must get my lamp back!"

It took months for the wicked magician to make his way to the city where Aladdin lived. By this time, the princess was expecting their first child and stayed mainly indoors. When the magician asked about Aladdin, he learned that he had gone hunting for a few days and was directed to the magnificent palace beside the sultan's. The magician was convinced that Aladdin had the lamp. He now had to concoct a clever plan to retrieve it while Aladdin was away.

The next day, the magician, dressed in the shabby clothes of a street vendor and carrying a basket of shiny new brass lamps, stood under the windows of the palace and shouted loudly: "New lamps for old! New lamps for old!"

One of the maidservants heard him and rushed to the princess, laughing. "Can you imagine the folly of this man, your highness, selling new lamps for old! I wonder how he makes any profit."

The princess, who had a good heart, looked around the room. She caught sight of the magic lamp sitting on a shelf, gathering dust. "Why don't you take him this one?" she suggested to the maidservant. "We never seem to use it."

So the maidservant took the old lamp and handed it over. The magician could not believe his luck. He waited until nighttime. Then he took the lamp and rubbed it with a bit of sand. Immediately the genie appeared in a cloud of smoke, bellowing: "Shabbey, Labbey, your slave is here to obey! I am the genie of the lamp, your wish is my command!"

"I order you to carry Aladdin's palace with the princess in it to my home in Africa."

Within minutes, the beautiful palace and its terrified occupants landed in the middle of the African jungle, followed by the wicked magician on a flying carpet.

The following morning, the sultan decided to call upon his daughter for breakfast. But, to his horror, there was no palace to be seen, let alone his darling Badr el Boudour.

"Bring me my son-in-law immediately!" shouted the angry sultan. "Allah only knows what he's up to."

Aladdin, returning from his hunting expedition, was speechless with shock as he rode toward the sultan's palace.

"Bring me back my daughter at once!" bellowed the sultan. "Or you will pay for this with your life!"

"Give me forty days, my lord, and she will be back," promised Aladdin. And without further ado, he galloped out of the city in search of his beloved princess.

That night, Aladdin stopped by a well to drink, wash and pray. As he rubbed his hands together, partly in prayer, partly in worry, he accidentally brushed the magic ring. Immediately the genie of the ring appeared and said: "Shabbey, Labbey, your slave is here to obey! I am the genie of the ring, ask of me anything."

"Bring me back my palace and my wife," cried Aladdin.

"I cannot do so, master," said the genie of the ring. "Only the genie of the lamp can do that, for he is much more powerful than me."

"Then take me to her immediately," said Aladdin, and within minutes he was flying toward Africa.

As they landed beneath the princess's window, he heard her shout: "I shall not leave this room until you tell me what you've done to my husband!"

"Your husband is dead and buried," the wicked magician replied. "Your father had him executed when you disappeared."

"That's not true," cried the princess. "I am not leaving this room until you give me proof of that."

Aladdin was relieved to find his wife in such a combative mood. "I must first go and speak to her then work out how to get the magic lamp back," he said to himself. "Take me to the princess," he commanded, and in an instant he was standing next to his wife, who almost fainted with joy to see him alive.

"Shhh," he whispered. "I am so glad you are unhurt. We must find a way of getting the magic lamp back."

"I have an idea," said the princess. "Why don't I pretend I have changed my mind and let the wicked magician into my room, then offer him a drink with sleeping powder in it?"

"Genie of the ring," said Aladdin, "bring me some sleeping powder this instant."

The genie obeyed, reappearing within seconds with the powder. Badr el Boudour asked her maidservants to prepare the most delicious sherbet and slipped the powder into one cup. Aladdin hid in a closet and waited for the magician to return. Soon, they heard his steps approaching.

"Princess," he wheedled, "I beg you to change your mind. Aladdin is truly dead. I shall have the proof tomorrow."

"If this is the case," murmured Badr el Boudour in her sweetest voice, "let me invite you in for a glass of sherbet."

The wicked magician could not believe his luck, for when the princess finally opened her door she looked more beautiful than the moon.

"Welcome," she said. "Take this — you must be thirsty."

"More thirsty for a sight of you," he said, gulping down his sherbet, his eyes glued to her. After just a few mouthfuls, he was snoring away on the couch. The princess soon found the lamp hidden away in a pocket in his robes.

"Aladdin, come here quickly," she called. "I have your lamp!"

Aladdin jumped out of the closet, took his beloved lamp and rubbed it at once. Out popped the genie, with his customary greeting: "Shabbey, Labbey, your slave is here to obey! I am the genie of the lamp, your wish is my command!" Then he added: "I am so relieved to be serving you again, sir."

"Take us back, and the palace as well, but leave the magician here. We never wish to see him again."

So the genie carried the palace and its inhabitants back, and as the sultan woke up and looked out of his window, he was overjoyed to see his daughter and her husband walking toward his palace, smiling and holding hands.

"They're back, they're back!" said the sultan to his wife. "Hurry up, my dear, and get dressed, I want to hear the full story!"

The Diamond Anklet

Zubaida was the youngest of three half sisters and the most beautiful. The three girls were born of different mothers and when their mothers died, the sisters lived alone. Zubaida worked as a carpet weaver. She sat at her loom every day with a smile on her face and a tune on her lips, while the most intricate designs sprang from her nimble fingers. Her two sisters did nothing. They simply spent the money Zubaida earned.

The two elder sisters were jealous of Zubaida's beauty. In truth, she was simply remarkable, with long brown hair that swayed like palm leaves and green, almond-shaped eyes. Her lips were as bright as the ripe seeds of a pomegranate and her feet as delicate as a gazelle's. What is more, she had a lovely personality. She was also the best carpet weaver in town, working from morning until night without a word of complaint.

Although Zubaida's carpets fetched a lot of money in the souk, her sisters only let her keep a few dirhams with which she bought flowers for her room or a comb for her

43

hair or a small piece of cake, for she was often hungry.

One day, Zubaida met a strange old man in the souk. He wore a simple turban and had a long white beard. He held out to her a small clay jar. "This little pot will bring you happiness, my child," he said.

"How can a simple clay jar bring happiness?" asked Zubaida with a laugh as she offered him her dirhams.

"Just take it home and you will see," said the old man mysteriously.

Back home, Zubaida put some flowers in the jar and returned to her carpet weaving. She was now feeling hungry. "I wish ..." she began.

The words were hardly out of her mouth when she heard a deep voice inside the jar saying: "Ask for what you wish and you will have it."

Zubaida jumped up. She turned the jar around and around, but she could not see anything in it except her flowers and the water. "I must be hearing things," she told herself. "I wish I had enough money left for a date cake."

In an instant, some delicious date cakes appeared in front of her. Zubaida could not contain her joy. She started to twirl around the room with her platter of freshly baked cakes. Then she sat down to eat them quietly before her sisters returned.

From that day on, Zubaida's life started to change. Whenever her sisters went out, she asked the genie in her little clay jar for special favors: dresses, shawls and jewels; delicately embroidered slippers; delicious dishes of rice and meat; and the best woolen threads with which to weave her carpets. She always made sure she shared her gifts, however, distributing them among her neighbors. She also made sure she kept the magic

45

jar secret from her sisters, changing back into her old and tattered clothes before they came home.

One day, the Shah decided to invite all the young people to his palace to celebrate his son's coming of age.

"You cannot go in those worn-out old clothes," her sisters told Zubaida. "You would shame us all. You had better stay here, taking care of the house instead." Poor Zubaida was lost for words. But the moment her sisters had left, she went straight to her faithful little clay jar. "Please make me a dress the color of the moon," she whispered. Immediately, a shimmering silk robe appeared, with a matching veil and slippers.

"All I need now is some beautiful diamond anklets and bracelets," she told her jar. And they too appeared. When she put them on, they made the loveliest tinkling sound.

Zubaida hurried to the party. When she entered the women's quarters, all of the ladies gasped with admiration. "Who is this mysterious lady?" they asked. "Where does she come from?" Even her sisters did not recognize her behind her fine veil.

Zubaida spent the time asking discreet questions about the Shah's son. She soon learned that he was an outstanding young man, hardworking and generous, and that his favorite pastimes were hunting, playing polo and chess. She tasted delicious foods served on silver platters, drank from crystal goblets. When she danced everyone noticed her diamond anklets and bracelets, which sparkled at every step.

Zubaida almost forgot the time, so happy was she. But suddenly she overheard her sisters saying their good-byes. She hurried to a side door and ran as fast as she could down the palace steps to reach home before them.

She took off her anklets to avoid making any noise, but in her haste she dropped one of them into a water trough by the palace stables. Then she hurried home, hid the dress and pretended to be fast asleep.

"You missed an amazing party," drawled the two sisters the next morning. "There was a mysterious lady in a dress the color of the moon and she danced like a gazelle. You should have seen the jewelry she had on," they sighed. "It would take you a lifetime of weaving to be able to afford just one of her anklets. Shouldn't you be working now?"

As Zubaida sat at her loom, a prince's groom brought one of the Shah's horses to drink at the water trough. The moment the horse saw the shining anklet in the water, he neighed in fright. The groom spotted the diamond anklet. He took it straight to the palace.

"Ah!" said the Shah's wife. "There was a lovely young woman with a dress the color of the moon and beaded silver slippers. She danced like a gazelle. I seem to remember she was wearing diamond anklets, just like this one."

"Mother!" cried the prince. "You must find her for me. She could be the bride I am looking for!"

"Let's not rush things, my child," said his mother. "We won't know until we see her. I shall ask your father to order a search for the mysterious lady who has lost this anklet."

So the Shah sent the royal guards together with the royal maidservants to knock at every door in the city.

When they reached Zubaida's house, the royal maidservants tried to attach the anklet to the first sister's ankle, then to the second sister's, but with no success.

"Don't you have another sister?" asked one of the maidservants, who happened to know the family well. "The one that makes beautiful carpets."

"What do you want with her?" said the sisters. "She never leaves her loom, and besides, she has the ugliest feet you've ever seen."

"The prince has instructed us to try the anklet on all the women of the kingdom," replied the maidservant, "and he means everyone. Go and fetch your younger sister, please!"

So they did. You should have seen the look of horror on their faces when they found Zubaida wearing her moon-colored dress and her beaded silver slippers.

The maidservants instantly remembered the beautiful young woman who had danced so well at the party. Of course, the anklet was just the right size and was a perfect match to the one Zubaida already had on.

The maidservants wailed with joy and declared Zubaida to be the eagerly-awaited royal bride. Leaving the older sisters gaping, they escorted her to the palace. The Shah and queen were captivated, as was the prince, who fell instantly in love with her, and arrangements were made for the royal wedding.

Now, as everyone was preparing for the wedding celebrations, Zubaida's two sisters were searching her room inch by inch for the secret of her moon-colored dress and her jewelry. All they could find was the old clay jar and some jewelry.

"Let's pretend to be happy for her and take her belongings to the palace," said one sister to the other. "Maybe we shall discover her secret that way."

Zubaida welcomed her sisters with forgiveness and open arms. She insisted that they come to the wedding and she even offered to have special dresses made for them.

"We are very grateful for your generosity, little sister," they cooed. "We are truly happy for you, and wish you a wonderful life. We have just one question. Do you still need the little clay jar in your room and the jewels we have found under your mattress?"

"You can keep them all. I have no need of my little clay jar anymore now that my prince will provide for all my needs." Then Zubaida blurted out: "I can even tell you the secret of the jar!" And with that, she told them all about the genie.

Now the sisters had everything they needed. The moment they returned home, they asked the magic jar for half a dozen poisoned hairpins, decorated with diamonds.

On the morning of the wedding, the sisters took their poisoned gift to the palace in a beautiful golden filigree box and presented it to Zubaida. "We were hoping to put them in your hair ourselves," they told her, in their sweetest voices.

"Of course, dear ones," said Zubaida good-heartedly. But the moment the first pin touched her scalp, Zubaida felt dizzy. With the second she fainted into her sisters' arms. The malicious pair continued planting the pins into their sister's hair. They did not manage to kill her; instead, the poison transformed her into a white dove with six diamond pins hidden under the soft white feathers of its head.

"There," cackled the wicked sisters, after they had finished their gruesome task. "Go and marry your prince now!" The dove flew out of the window and perched on top of a nearby tree, trembling with fear. Then the sisters threw open the doors of the dressing room and ran toward the palace guards, shouting, weeping and tearing their clothes. "Help, help, the bride has disappeared!"

The guards searched the palace. The Shah dispatched his soldiers to the furthest frontiers of the kingdom. The queen's maidservants were sent into every home to look for Zubaida, but she was nowhere to be found.

The prince fell sick with heartache. He stopped eating; he no longer went hunting or played chess or visited his friends. He just sat by the window of his room and prayed to Allah for the safe return of his bride. His only comfort was a beautiful white dove with soft, shiny feathers, which cooed on his windowsill.

One morning as the dove lingered by his window, the prince gently caressed its soft head. It did not fly away; on the contrary it stood still, as if wanting more. So he caressed its head again, until his fingers touched something hard.

"I must find out what it is," he told himself. He gently lifted the feathers on the dove's head and saw six shiny diamonds stuck deep into the bird's scalp. As he lifted the first one, the dove fainted in his hands but he continued to remove each

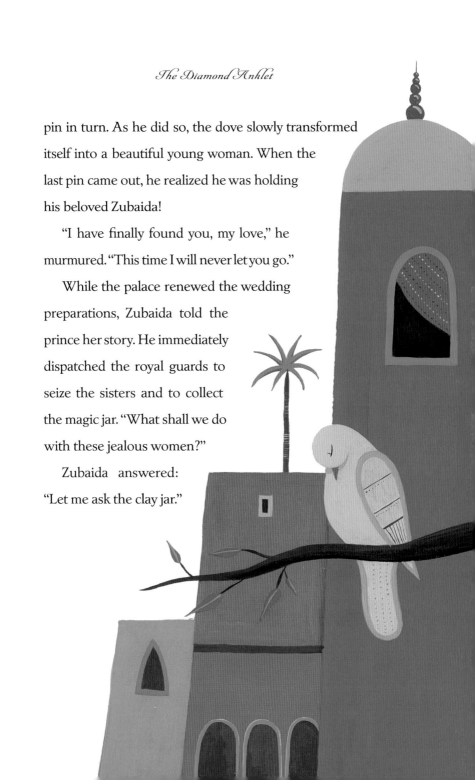

pin in turn. As he did so, the dove slowly transformed itself into a beautiful young woman. When the last pin came out, he realized he was holding his beloved Zubaida!

"I have finally found you, my love," he murmured. "This time I will never let you go."

While the palace renewed the wedding preparations, Zubaida told the prince her story. He immediately dispatched the royal guards to seize the sisters and to collect the magic jar. "What shall we do with these jealous women?"

Zubaida answered: "Let me ask the clay jar."

By now, the genie living in the jar was utterly worn out from having to indulge every whim of the two greedy sisters. By way of a reply, he simply stretched out his arms, caught one sister in each arm and pulled them into the jar, swallowing them both in one big gulp.

"We shall put this jar on the top shelf of the treasury," the Prince declared. "With the poisoned pins inside," he added. "No one will disturb it, I am sure, for our treasurer has better things to do than notice an old clay pot."

The day of the wedding ceremony was declared a national holiday, and Allah gave the prince and his bride many happy years together as well as half a dozen children — who loved nothing more than listening to the story of how their parents met and playing with their mother's diamond anklets.

Jullanar of the Sea

In a city of ancient Persia there once lived a great shah. He was a wise and good man who ruled justly, so that all his subjects wished him a long and happy life.

Now, this shah was blessed in every way except one. He had no wife, and no heir. He prayed every day for a woman who would give him a son or daughter, but although he was already growing long in years, he had not yet met anyone with whom he could share his life. Then one day a merchant from a distant land came to the city and everything changed.

The merchant brought with him a slave girl. When he presented her to the shah, the shah was speechless, for she was as beautiful as the rising moon and as slender as a reed. Her silky black hair flowed down her back. Her cheeks were as lustrous as ripe pomegranates and her dark eyes shone with warmth.

The good shah's heart trembled. "How much do you want for this girl?" he asked.

"I have been traveling for over a year to present her to your majesty," answered the merchant, "and I paid a very high price for her. I am asking you for two thousand dinars, sire."

"That sum does not reflect her true worth," declared the shah. And turning to his vizier, he said: "Give this man not two but ten thousand dinars, and while you're at it, make sure he gets a new robe and a decent meal."

The merchant bowed low, kissed the shah's hand and left.

The shah gave the slave girl the best rooms in the palace. For reasons he could not quite explain to himself, he felt sure that she would be happiest in rooms overlooking the sea. When he paid his first visit to her, she was indeed standing by the window, staring out across the waves. But whenever he tried to engage her in conversation, she remained completely silent. This state of affairs continued for a full year. At first, the quiet shah was agitated by her behavior, but then he began to enjoy her silent charm.

When the anniversary of her arrival came around, he tried one more time: "My lady, if you are able to speak, in the name of Allah, please let me hear your voice, if only once."

The girl lifted her head, smiled and in a voice that was as clear as it was gentle, she said: "O great and gallant Shah, your wish is my command. May Allah give you a long life and make all your wishes come true. I wish to inform you that I am now pregnant with your child."

The shah rushed to embrace her. "This is a great day indeed!" he declared. "First to hear you speak, secondly to know I will finally have my own child to love and cherish."

And with a swish of his robes, he went to announce the good news and he called on the sheikh to arrange a marriage.

That evening, the shah returned to his wife and asked her gently: "Tell me, my dear, what is your name and why have you not spoken a word to me until today?"

"My name is Jullanar of the Sea," she answered "and I am the daughter of a sea king. When my father died he left his kingdom to my brother Saleh. But we quarreled and I left, vowing never to return. I was sitting weeping by the shore when a man saw me, took me with him against my will and sold me to the slave merchant. The rest of the story you know. If you had not been so kind to me during this past year, I would have returned to the sea."

"But my dear, why did you wait so long to tell me all this?" asked the shah.

"I wanted to make sure that you would be a good father to this baby. Now I know that you will. And as my confinement is near, I feel I should like my mother and brother by my side. May I invite them to come and visit?"

"Of course," he replied. "Invite them here immediately."

So Jullanar removed a bead of her pearl necklace, threw it into the fire, then muttered a magic incantation. The sea outside the window started to foam and billow and out of the waves emerged an elegant old lady, a handsome man and five beautiful maidens. These were Jullanar's mother, brother and cousins. The shah enjoyed getting to know his unexpected and exotic new relatives.

When the baby was born, it was a beautiful boy. Jullanar's mother bathed him and dressed him and carried him through the palace to present him. The joyful shah knelt down and thanked Allah in front of the whole court.

"Badr will be his name," he said, "for it signifies the moon, and he is as beautiful as the moon when it is full." Then he declared there should be forty days and forty nights of celebrations. It was the happiest day of his life.

On the fortieth day, as Queen Jullanar was sitting with her husband and family, playing with the baby, her brother Saleh took the child

in his arms, twirled him around
the room and cooed to him in
a strange language. Then he
suddenly flew out of the window
and disappeared with the baby into the
sea. The shah felt the world turn dark
and let out a loud cry: "Bring him back,
bring back my son!"

"Do not be afraid," said Queen Jullanar. "My brother will
not harm the child."

So they sat waiting by the window, silently praying for
the safe return of their child until they heard the sea foam
and surge and looked to see the boy's uncle appearing out
of the waves holding the baby in his arms. Thanking
Allah silently, they waited for Saleh to explain himself.

"I hope you were not frightened, your majesty," said
Saleh, bowing before the shah as he passed the infant back
to his father. "I went to the sea to draw around my nephew's
eyes with special kohl blessed by the words inscribed on the
seal of King Solomon, son of David."

Queen Jullanar then explained to her husband how, whenever a child was born to the people of the sea, the parents drew around its eyes in order to ward off evil.

Now Saleh took a purse from his pocket and emptied it in front of the shah, scattering scores of emeralds, rubies and diamonds at his feet, and saying: "Brother-in-law, these gems are gifts for your son Badr from his Uncle Saleh. May he never be in need."

The shah was deeply touched by the generous gift and invited Saleh to extend his stay, but his guest replied: "The kingdom of the sea awaits me. However, you are welcome to stay with us whenever you want, and we shall gladly come and visit you as often as we can." With that, he and his mother and five cousins took their leave.

There were many visits from the people of the sea while Prince Badr was growing up. The years flew by and soon he was a fine young man, handsome, clever and courteous. He spoke many languages and chanted verses of the Koran exceptionally well. He was also an excellent rider, archer, sailor and poet.

When Prince Badr turned eighteen and had learned all that was needed to be a good king, his father summoned his court and announced to them he was ready to retire and that Prince Badr was to be his chosen heir. Badr was as good a ruler as his father, dividing his days between sporting pursuits and affairs of the state. He often traveled through the cities and provinces of his kingdom, listening to his subjects and helping them.

But not long after he had become shah, Badr was called back to the palace with the news that his father was dying. The old shah just had time to give his son one last blessing before he passed peacefully away.

When Badr turned twenty-one, his uncle Saleh came to visit him, bearing magnificent presents of coral and pearls. A sumptuous party was held and everyone danced until dawn. As the guests took their leave, Saleh approached Queen Jullanar to speak with her privately.

"My dear sister," he said. "Don't you think it's high time we found your son a bride? As your only child, if anything happened to him the kingdom would be in great danger, and so would you."

"Who do you suggest, my dear brother?" asked the queen.

"There are many worthy princesses in the kingdom of the sea," answered Saleh. "However, I think that none is more worthy of my nephew than Princess Jawhara."

"Describe her to me," said the queen.

"She matches your son in beauty and talent. She has no equal among the princesses of the sea or the land. When she smiles the sea anemones open their petals and the fish dance in the water," replied Saleh.

"Now I remember her," said Jullanar. "Her mother used to be my friend when I was a child. Your suggestion is perfect. How shall we introduce them to each other?"

"First, we have to convince Jawhara's father," said Saleh. "He has a reputation for being vain and tyrannical. I suggest we don't tell Badr about our plan just yet."

What they did not know was that Badr had overheard their conversation. After the party, he had taken a walk in the garden. Hearing voices coming from his mother's sitting room, he had hidden by the window and listened. The description of Princess Jawhara's beauty roused his curiosity, and when his mother had retired to bed, he could not resist accosting his uncle: "I beg you to take me with you tomorrow to the kingdom of the sea so I can meet this princess."

"Didn't your mother teach you not to listen to people's conversations?" Saleh admonished him.

"Dear uncle, I know I am in the wrong," replied Badr. "Forgive me, I heard you speaking by chance. Please take me with you tomorrow to the kingdom of the sea."

"In that case, we must tell your mother at once," said his uncle.

"Let's not worry her unnecessarily," said Badr. "I shall leave a message with my vizier that I have gone away on business.

At dawn the next day, Badr strode down to a sea that was as blue as lapis lazuli. His uncle arrived soon afterwards and the two men embraced. "Take this ring," said Saleh to his nephew. "It will protect you from evil."

With these words, he took his nephew by the hand and walked with him into the waves. They swam down and down until they reached Saleh's kingdom.

"Welcome to the kingdom of the sea, grandson," said Saleh's mother. "Come and tell us your news."

"Guess what?" said her son teasingly.

"Your grandson is in love!"

His mother raised an inquisitive eyebrow: "Aha! And may I know with whom?"

"With none other than Princess Jawhara, daughter of King Shamandal," replied Saleh.

"She is indeed matchless," said his mother, "but it won't be easy to win her father. I know what we can do, however. I shall go to the treasury."

The next day, Saleh and his mother set out for the palace of King Shamandal. They took with them six sea horses

66

carrying caskets filled with precious jewels and a retinue of one thousand men, partly for show and partly for protection.

"I have come to ask for your daughter's hand for my nephew," said Saleh, saluting King Shamandal. "And as a token of our esteem, my mother has chosen to offer you some of the finest jewels in our treasury," he continued, kneeling to present Shamandal with one of the caskets.

"My daughter is not for sale," snapped the king. "And she does not need your jewels," he added, dismissing them with a wave of his hand. His guests had no choice but to leave.

Saleh was fuming, however. "I cannot tolerate such insulting behavior from another person, let alone a king!" he exclaimed. "What would my subjects think? That they too can be rude to me!" With these words he summoned the soldiers of his retinue and ordered them to storm the palace, taking Shamandal prisoner.

As for Princess Jawhara, when word reached her that her father had been taken captive, she fled with her favorite maidservant. A small fishing boat took the two of them to a nearby island where the princess hid in a tree house.

Meanwhile, when Badr's grandmother and uncle did not return, he decided to search for them. He set out in a small fishing boat and rowed for several hours until Fate brought him to the very island where Princess Jawhara was hiding. He even took a nap underneath the tree house!

When he woke from his sleep, Badr looked up through the tree branches to see a lovely face peering down at him. "This beauty matches exactly the description my uncle gave of Princess Jawhara," he thought. "She truly is perfect."

After an embarrassed silence, he said to the face peering down from the tree: "Hello! My name is Badr. What's yours?"

"My name is Jawhara and I am the daughter of King Shamandal. Our palace has been overtaken by a strange army and my father imprisoned. I have had to flee."

"Princess Jawhara?" thought Badr, unable to believe his ears. "I am sure it is my uncle Saleh's army that has conquered her palace. How can I ask for her hand now?" Then, plucking up his courage, he said: "Princess Jawhara, I fear this is all my fault. My uncle Saleh had gone to ask for your hand on my behalf. Now I hear that he has taken your father prisoner and conquered your palace. I am truly sorry," he added.

"What does it matter whether you are sorry or not!"

retorted Princess Jawhara, who was beside herself with rage and despair at this turn of events. "It is clearly your fault that my beloved father is a prisoner and I am homeless."

"Let us go and tell my uncle to release your father," said Badr, by now totally smitten.

As she glared back at him, Jawhara formed a plan. "First, you will have to climb up here and help me down," she said, "then perhaps we'll see if we can resolve this little difficulty."

But as soon as they touched, her face became as cold as marble and she said in a strange, harsh voice: "Away from me, enemy! Lose your human form and become a bird!"

With these words, Badr was transformed into a beautiful bird with a blue beak and blue feet. He perched shivering on a branch of the tree.

"Catch him at once!" Princess Jawhara commanded her maidservant, "and take him to the Dry Island where he will die slowly and painfully of hunger and thirst."

But the maidservant, who secretly felt sorry for Badr, took him instead to the Isle of Plenty. Here a multitude of fruit trees grew, watered by the sweetest of streams. "At least you will be well fed here, my handsome one," said the girl, caressing the bird's head.

Badr, transformed into a bird, was let loose on the Isle of Plenty. His distraught uncle searched for him everywhere. As for his anxious mother Jullanar, she swam to her mother and brother to ask if they knew of her son's whereabouts.

"I am so sorry, my dear sister," said Saleh. "I should have told you about our plan to visit the kingdom of the sea." Then he told her the story of the failed marriage request and of Badr's mysterious disappearance. "There is no point in you waiting for him here," he went on. "You should go back to Persia and govern the kingdom while he is away. I am sure that Allah in his infinite wisdom will guide you."

So Queen Jullanar took leave of her brother and mother, and returned to Persia to wait for her son, taking over as ruler of the country in his absence.

As for Badr, he spent his days pecking at fruits and learning how to live in the wild, until one day a hunter trapped him in his net and put him in a cage. "What an exquisite bird," he thought to himself. "I must take it as a present to the king."

The King of the Isle of Plenty was captivated by the bird. He fed him at his table and was astonished to see Badr eating like a human: hopping from plate to plate, choosing the most tender morsels of meat, even pecking at the dessert!

"What a strange bird," the king told his wife. "He eats everything I eat. How do you explain that?"

The Queen of the Isle of Plenty looked closely at Badr and said: "This bird is not a bird but a human. Someone must have cast a spell on him."

"Madam," said the king, "you cannot be serious!"

"I am perfectly serious, my lord," she replied. "This is Shah Badr of Persia and his mother is Queen Jullanar of the Sea. Follow me to my rooms and you will see."

"My dear, you never cease to amaze me," said the king.

The queen of the Isle of Plenty was in fact a powerful magician. She was so moved by the plight of handsome Shah Badr that she decided to free him from the spell. So she took a copper vessel, filled it with water and pronounced some magic words over it. The water began to boil, bubble and steam. The queen then sprinkled some of the water onto the feathers of the shivering bird. In an instant, the blue feathers fell off and Badr returned to his human form. He fell on his knees to kiss the hands of the powerful queen, while the king looked on in amazement.

"Come, let us sit and enjoy a refreshing cup of sherbet," said the king, "while you tell us what we can do to help you."

"I should be grateful for a boat to take me back to the land of Persia, where my absence must have caused great pain to my mother and disruption to my kingdom," said Badr.

"Your wish is granted," replied the king, ordering one of his newest ships to set sail with his best captain and sailors.

For the first ten days the ship sailed smoothly across a sea that was as bright and calm as a mirror. But on the eleventh day, the wind changed and a storm arose, tossing the ship in all directions until it hit a rock and split in two. Some of the sailors drowned; the others, including Badr, clung to pieces of wreckage until they reached the shore.

Badr dragged himself onto the sand. "Thanks be to Allah," he thought, "I am back on dry land." As he lay there, exhausted and hungry, he looked around and saw, rising before him, the walls of a great white city. Passing through the city gates, Badr was struck by all the animals wandering around — horses, asses, cows and camels — but scarcely a fellow human being. At every step, one of these creatures would stand in his path, as if deliberately blocking his way.

"What is wrong with these animals?" he said to himself.

Finally, he came across an old man sitting by his vegetable stall and smiling kindly through his wrinkles. "Good day to you, uncle," said Badr, saluting the man.

"Good day to you, handsome youth," said the old man, who was struck by Badr's good grace and pleasant demeanor. "What brings you to our shores? Can I offer you a cup of sweet tea?"

Exhausted from lack of food and sleep, Badr sat by the vegetable stall, sipping the delicious hot tea, and told the old man his story.

"Praise be to Allah," said the old man, whose name was Abdallah. "Your mother must have prayed hard for you to have escaped evil so often."

"I am sure she has," answered Badr.

"I hope she continues praying for you, my child, for I am afraid your ordeals are not yet over. You have reached the City of Enchantments, ruled by a wicked sorceress called Queen Sahar, who transforms anyone who opposes her into a horse, ass, cow or camel."

Badr was beginning to understand. "Can you tell me why these animals were trying to stop me from going further into the city?" he asked.

"They were trying to shield you from the queen's guards stationed at her palace," replied old Abdallah. "If they see you, they will seize you and take you before the queen, where she will turn you into an animal like everyone else."

"What should I do?" asked Badr anxiously.

"I shall pretend that you are my nephew here on a visit," said Abdallah. "The queen is very fond of me because I provide her with the best fruit and vegetables. This will give us both time to think of a way for you to leave the city without being found out."

"I am already in your debt," said Badr, asking permission to help himself to a delicious mango from the stall.

A month passed before Sahar, Queen of the City of Enchantments, realized she had a visitor. During that time, Badr lived with old Abdallah like a son, helping him run the stall, preparing his meals and sitting with him in the evenings, recounting the stories that his mother Jullanar had told him as a child.

One afternoon, Queen Sahar stopped by Abdallah's stall and came face to face with Badr. "Tell me, Uncle Abdallah, who is this handsome young man?" she asked sweetly.

"This is my nephew, your majesty," answered the old man. "My late brother's son, who has come to visit me after his father's death."

"I wish to invite him to my palace for a meal," said the queen. "I shall send my men at noon tomorrow to escort him," said the queen with a smile.

"Your invitation is a privilege and a delight," lied Abdallah.

As soon as the queen had disappeared from view, he apologized to Badr: "My son, it is impossible for anyone to refuse the queen. She is a most powerful sorceress. I advise you to keep your eyes and ears open and use your wits. Never underestimate the power of clear thinking," he added, giving Badr a hug to reassure him.

The next morning, Queen Sahar dispatched her men to collect Badr. He rode through the streets on a magnificent stallion with a white star on its forehead. As he passed, everyone stopped whatever they were doing and gasped in admiration, for Badr was truly as handsome as the full moon and he rode like a king. Riding by, he could hear the remarks of the crowd — "Poor man, does he know how cruel and wicked our queen is?" or "Will anyone deliver us from her?" At the palace he was received with great pomp and given a place of honor at the queen's banquet. After the meal, Badr was shown to a comfortable guest room and invited to stay for the evening concert when the most talented musicians and poets would sing to the guests or recite poetry.

In this way, a routine started which continued for many days: in the early morning, a walk in the palace gardens with the queen, followed by a delicious breakfast; at mid-morning, riding in the nearby hills; then lunch, then a siesta, then card games or chess, then dinner and a concert.

After a month, Badr had changed his mind about the queen. "I don't understand what the fuss is all about," he told himself, as he prepared for their morning stroll.

On that very morning, the queen had dispatched a servant to say that she could not join her guest. So Badr went off by himself around the gardens until he reached the queen's quarters. Standing to one side of the tall windows, he peeped inside and saw her kneading bread with flour she had ground and had kept locked in a special box, along with a secret assortment of spices and other magical ingredients.

"This is what I shall feed you tonight, you handsome and foolish youth," she was chanting.

A cold chill ran through Badr's spine. He went straight to the stables, called for his horse and said to his servant: "Please inform the queen that I am missing my Uncle Abdallah so much that I must visit him instantly. I shall be back this evening."

"Dear uncle," he said, as he dismounted, "I saw something I should not have seen. The queen was kneading bread in her room and singing as she worked. Do you have any idea what this bread is?"

"My son, you are very wise to have come away," replied Abdallah. "The bread is magical. She feeds it to people to transform them into horses, asses, cows or camels."

"What can I do?" asked Badr, panicking. "She is expecting me back to dine with her this very evening."

"Don't worry," said old Abdallah with a smile. "She is not the only one in this town who can make magic bread. Come, roll up your sleeves so that you too may learn."

So Badr helped old Abdallah knead and bake several small loaves of bread to which the old man added a good dose of his own magic, for he too was a sorcerer who knew how to use his skills when the occasion demanded.

"Here," said Abdallah, presenting a basket full of bread to Badr, "take these loaves and offer them to the queen at tonight's meal. But remember! Do not eat one morsel of her bread; instead, tease her and cajole her until she accepts some of yours."

"Thank you, uncle, for your advice and your help" said Badr, hugging his old friend. "I shall see you tomorrow."

"May Allah protect you, my son," said the old man.

When Badr reached the palace, the queen was waiting for him impatiently. "What took you so long?" she asked.

"I apologize, your majesty," he replied. "I have been helping my uncle to bake bread for you. He wishes to thank you for all your hospitality toward me."

"But we have bread in the palace," said the queen, frowning. "I too have baked some fresh loaves."

"Ah! I bet they are not quite as delicious as my uncle's," said Badr, with his charming smile. "Do try one? They are hot from the oven."

"No, no, no — I had much rather you try mine," insisted the queen.

"Of course," answered Badr, pretending to eat the crust but secretly slipping it into his pocket.

Then, pouring some water from a jar into the palm of her hand, the queen sprinkled it on to Badr's face and said: "Be transformed into an ugly, limping donkey this instant!"

"What was that you said?" he queried innocently, eyes wide.

"I was just joking," she said with a shrug.

"You frightened me for a moment, your majesty," said Badr offering her one of his loaves. "Now it's your turn to taste some of Uncle Abdallah's delicious baking."

This time the queen could not refuse. But the moment she swallowed the bread, she began to writhe like a serpent. "What have you put in this bread?" she hissed. And before Badr could answer, she had become a beautiful mare.

"I think I prefer you this way," said Badr, laughing. "And I'm taking you to my uncle immediately." With these words, he put a bridle around the mare's neck and dragged her kicking and neighing back to old Abdallah's vegetable stall.

"Vile sorceress!" said Abdallah when he saw the mare. "You finally got what you deserve." Then, turning to Badr, he said: "My lord, you have no reason to stay in this city a moment longer. Mount the mare and go back to your kingdom. Your mother and your subjects need you."

After embracing the old man, Badr rode for three days until he came to a city where an old man with a white beard invited him to have a glass of lemonade and take a rest. Being a trusting person, Badr accepted the old man's hospitality. An old woman served them. When she saw the beautiful mare, she exclaimed: "Young man, please sell me this mare. It looks exactly like the one my son has lost."

"Old lady," said Badr politely, "this mare is not for sale."

"Not even for one thousand gold pieces?" she asked.

Badr laughed: "Maybe one thousand gold pieces would make me change my mind."

At that, the old woman unwrapped her belt and took out one thousand shiny gold pieces.

"I was just joking," said Badr.

But the old man said: "Didn't you know, young man, that in our town our word is our bond? If you value your life, you must sell the mare for the price you have agreed."

So Badr reluctantly took the money and gave the mare away. The moment the old woman had picked up the reins, she embraced the mare, whispering: "My daughter, my darling, I have missed you so so much." Then, sprinkling the mare with water, she ordered: "Return to your human shape."

The Queen of the City of Enchantments appeared instantly and hugged her mother. Badr could not believe his eyes nor fully understand how cleverly he had been tricked until he heard a low whistle and a huge genie appeared. "Ladies, I am in your hands," the genie announced, bowing in front of the two women.

"Take us to the City of Enchantments," ordered Queen Sahar. Within minutes, Badr was flying on the genie's shoulders back to the city. As soon as they alighted at the palace, the queen sprinkled him with magic water and said:

"Leave your human shape and become an owl this instant!"

Within seconds Badr had been transformed into an owl.

"Put him in a cage and starve him to death," ordered the queen.

Mercifully, the maidservant who took Badr away was also a good friend of old Abdallah. She secretly went to see the old man to tell him what had happened.

"It's time to use my magic again," said Abdallah. He then gave a whistle and a huge genie appeared in front of him, saying: "Shabbey, Labbey, your servant is here to obey."

"Lightning," Abdallah commanded, for this was the genie's name, "go at once to Persia and inform Queen Jullanar that her son is a prisoner of the Queen of the City of Enchantments. Let her gather an army of sea people to rescue her son from this evil woman."

"You say and I obey," Lightning the Genie answered.

Queen Jullanar was so overjoyed to hear that her son was alive that she went straight to her brother's kingdom. There, they summoned an army of sea people who rose

up into the air and flew behind the genie to the City of Enchantments. The army surrounded the palace of Queen Sahar and stormed the tower where the cage of Shah Badr was kept.

"My poor son," said Queen Jullanar, trembling with relief and rage as she opened the cage. "What have they done to you?" Then she sprinkled some magic water over the owl, transforming it back into human form.

"Let us go straight to old Abdallah to thank him for his help," said Jullanar, weeping with joy. "We must also reward Queen Sahar's maidservant for saving your life."

When these duties had been performed, Queen Jullanar flew back to Persia with Badr, carried by Lightning the Genie and followed by the army of sea people.

After a week of celebrations, Queen Jullanar took her son aside: "My son, I am getting old and I wish to see you married and with children. Let us try once more to find you a bride."

"Mother," answered Badr, kissing Queen Jullanar's hand, "I want to make you happy, but if the truth be told, I am still in love with Princess Jawhara whose father is a prisoner of Uncle Saleh."

"Let me see what I can do," said the queen.

"Saleh," she told her brother a short while afterwards, "please convince this prisoner of yours to give his daughter's hand to my son. I am getting old and I wish to see Badr married and with children before I say good-bye to this world."

"Dearest sister," said King Saleh, "you deserve to be a happy grandmother." With these words, he disappeared into the sea and went to talk to King Shamandal, who had become much better tempered, and considerably more likeable, after his spell in prison.

"Would you consider having your kingdom returned in exchange for the hand of your daughter to my nephew, Shah Badr?" asked Saleh.

"I admire your persistence," smiled King Shamandal. "But what if she says no?"

"It is up to you to convince her," said Saleh to his prisoner.

Princess Jawhara loved her father, but she was secretly very taken with Badr as well, so she was only too happy to help her father regain his kingdom. "I must be precious to be worth a kingdom," she whispered to Badr.

"You are my most precious jewel," he replied as he embraced her.

The Ebony Horse

The adventures of Prince Kamar el Akmar, or "Moon of Moons", began one afternoon in early autumn. It was the habit of his father, Shah Sabur of Persia, to open the gates of his palace twice a year, for the spring and autumn festivals. During these celebrations, the streets were sprinkled with rose petals, sweets were given to the children and everyone dressed in their finest clothes. Shah Sabur opened up his kitchens and his treasury, distributing food and money, dispensing justice and accepting greetings and gifts in return.

On this occasion, an Indian magician, skilled in making curious and rare inventions, presented the shah with a full-sized wooden horse carved in such a manner that it looked almost alive. Its coat shone, black as ebony, and it wore a finely crafted saddle and bridle, inlaid with golden studs and glittering jewels. Everyone marveled at its beauty.

"What is the purpose of this object?" asked Shah Sabur.

"Your majesty," the magician replied, bowing low, "when you mount this horse, it will carry you up into the air and take you wherever you want to go. Moreover, in a single day it will travel farther than you and I could travel in a year."

The shah was no fool, so he invited the magician to give a demonstration. And it was true! The horse could fly right around the palace. No one had ever seen anything like it.

"What would you like in return for your gift?" asked Sabur. "You may have whatever you wish for."

Now, the magician had heard of the beauty and grace of the shah's youngest daughter. So he told Sabur: "If you are truly pleased with my gift, your majesty, my wish is to ask for your youngest daughter's hand in marriage."

But the princess was horrified, the magician was old and ugly, with a nose like an eggplant and lips as pendulous as those of a camel. She ran to her room and threw herself on her bed, sobbing loudly. Her brother, who had just returned from a hunting expedition, heard her cries and rushed to her room. She told him everything.

The prince went straight to his father and confronted him. The shah shrugged. "Don't worry about your sister," he said. "Her suitor is quite worthy of her, no matter what he may look like." Then he showed his son the remarkable ebony horse and introduced him to the magician.

The prince was enchanted. He mounted
the horse straightaway. "How
does it work?" he asked. But
the magician, who was worried by this
turn of events, simply gave an enigmatic
smile and a deep bow. He was right to be concerned, for
as soon as Kamar el Akmar picked up the reins of the horse
it started to fly. Up, up, up it rose, above the roofs of the city,
high into the sky, and over mountains, hills and valleys.

Within a matter of minutes, the prince had disappeared
from sight.

"Bring him back!" demanded the shah.

But the magician replied, "Alas, your majesty, your son is
too impulsive. He has let the ebony horse fly too high and
too fast. There is nothing I can do."

Then the shah flew into a rage. He called his guards and had the magician taken to the dungeons.

At first, Kamar el Akmar was thrilled by the novelty of the flying horse. Then, realizing he knew neither how to bring it down, nor turn it around nor stop it, he began to panic. But, being a courageous and resourceful young man, he did not completely lose his nerve. Instead, he started twiddling the horse's ears and discovered that by doing this, he could control the horse, making it fly up and down and in different directions. As he drew closer to the earth he saw a magnificent palace surrounded by battlements and protected by many guards, dressed in chain mail and armed to the teeth.

"Hurrah!" he thought. "This looks like a good place to stop." But wanting to evade the guards, he steered the horse onto the roof. Then he went down one of the staircases, looking for food and drink as he had not eaten since the morning. Passing through a magnificent courtyard, he saw a light and went toward it. There he found a guard sleeping in front of a door, his hand on his sword. He silently took the guard's food bag off its hook and ate its contents, then he took his sword and quietly opened the door. The guard continued to snore away.

In the room, Kamar el Akmar was astonished to find a beautiful princess. She lay asleep on an ivory bed inlaid with jewels and draped with silk curtains embroidered with thousands of tiny pearls. He spent a long time just gazing at her. Then he could not resist any more. He drew back one of the curtains, leaned over and gave her a kiss on the cheek.

Straight away, the princess woke up and she was about to scream when she realized that the person standing by her bed was the most handsome young man she had ever seen. So she quickly recovered her wits, asked him who he was and sat up to listen to his story.

When Kamar el Akmar finished, the princess — whose name was Shams el Nahar, or "Day Sun" — introduced herself as the daughter of the King of Sanaa, in Yemen. Kamar el Akmar had flown a long way south in one day!

Hearing voices in the bedchamber, the princess's handmaiden raised the alarm. Kamar al Akmar was seized by the palace guards and brought before the king.

On learning that the intruder was a prince, the king was courteous to his unexpected guest and offered him a room for the night. But he was also so upset by the poor security in the palace that the next morning he challenged Kamar el

Akmar to prove he was indeed a king's son by fighting his whole army. Kamar el Akmar accepted, so the king ordered his commander in chief to prepare for battle. The army arrived on horseback, in full armor.

Seeing so many soldiers, Kamar el Akmar told the king: "It seems unfair that I should fight your army on foot when your men are all mounted on horses. I ask permission to use my horse, your majesty."

The king agreed to this, and Kamar el Akmar raced up the stairs to the roof, sprang into the saddle of the ebony horse and started twiddling its right ear. His mount swayed backward and forward then it began to rise, gliding slowly over the palace. By the time the soldiers had realized what was happening, the prince was high in the sky, waving down at them.

"Catch him! Catch the rogue!" cried the king. But his advisors restrained him. "Let him go, let him go," they said. "He must surely be a magician, so good riddance to him!" As for Shams el Nahar, she took to her chambers, refusing food and drink — for she had fallen deeply in love.

Kamar el Akmar flew like the wind until he reached his father's palace. Alighting on the roof, he saw that the stairs were strewn with ashes. "Oh! Someone important must have died," he thought. He found his entire family dressed in black and weeping, for they thought he had gone forever. They rushed over to him, their tears of grief turning to tears of joy. They sat him down to a good meal, demanding to hear all about his adventure. The prince then told them of his encounter with the beautiful Shams el Nahar, and of how he had narrowly escaped being killed by her father's soldiers.

While they sat there, eating, drinking and rejoicing, Shah Sabur asked one of the court singers to entertain them. She sang a poem of love and remembrance, her words moving Kamar el Akmar so much that he suddenly longed for the princess. So the moment the meal was finished, he excused himself. He climbed to the palace roof, mounted the ebony horse and flew all the way back to Yemen. There he found Shams el Nahar confined to her bed, pale and weak. She had not eaten a morsel since he had left.

Kamar el Akmar knelt at the princess's side and promised that he would come and visit her every week. But this was not enough for her. "Take me with you," she pleaded. "I cannot live without you any more." Then Shams el Nahar packed a casket, put on her loveliest silk dress, and quietly slipped away with Kamar el Akmar to the palace roof. They mounted the ebony horse and flew back across the starry sky to the kingdom of Persia.

As the young couple galloped through the night skies, Kamar el Akmar thought to himself: "I must show the princess how much I respect her. I should go alone to my father and announce her arrival properly." So he brought the ebony horse down by a small summer palace outside the city gates. He kissed the princess's hands and begged her to rest. Then he hurried away to announce his news and to organize a procession of welcome.

The magician had been released from prison following the prince's return. Having given up all hope of marrying the shah's daughter, he was determined to recover his precious ebony horse.

Walking by chance by the summer palace, he saw the horse and couldn't believe his luck.

The princess did not like the look of the magician one little bit. "Don't be afraid, your highness," he purred. "Prince Kamar el Akmar has sent me because I am the only one other than him who can fly the ebony horse. Besides," he continued, "he wouldn't want to send a handsome young man to accompany you on this journey, would he?"

"I suppose you are right," conceded the princess. Then, against her better judgement, she climbed onto the ebony horse with the magician behind her. No sooner had they begun to fly over the city than she saw a magnificent procession coming out of the shah's palace with a splendid litter mounted on top of an elephant. This must be the welcome procession, she realized. For a moment, she thought that the magician would bring the horse down to meet them, but to her horror the horse started flying higher.

"Stop, stop! What are you doing?" cried the princess.

"I am taking you away from the prince, who tricked me and took my horse. I am now your master!" said the magician.

"Oh no, you're not!" thought the princess, but how could she escape?

They flew all day until sunset. Then, as orange rays of sunlight bathed the evening sky, the magician brought them down to land in a rich green pasture near a forest. He ordered the princess to gather firewood while he rested.

Shams el Nahar went into the forest and started gathering twigs. Luckily for her, the King of Greece was riding by. He was intrigued when he saw a beautiful woman dressed in strange and expensive robes gathering wood like a peasant. Dismounting from his horse, he bowed low, introduced himself and asked the princess if she needed help. In a low voice, she told him her story, but she was careful not to mention that the ebony horse could fly.

The king sent his guards to seize the magician and carry the ebony horse back to his palace while he rode ahead with the princess. When they reached the palace, he gave her an entire wing of her own and provided many attendants to wait on her. As for the magician, he was put in prison. The ebony horse was taken to the treasury.

Shams el Nahar soon realized that the King of Greece had fallen in love with her and was determined to make her his wife. So she decided to pretend she was mad. When the servants came for her the next morning, she started pulling her hair, tearing her fine clothes and throwing her jewelry around the room. But the king said he would wait until she got better, for he was deeply smitten.

When Kamar el Akmar found out that his beloved Shams el Nahar and his precious ebony horse had both disappeared, he set out to search for them. For weeks he rode through the towns and villages of his father's kingdom, asking everyone he met whether they had seen an ebony horse or a beautiful princess. But they seemed to have disappeared like a mirage in the sand.

The young prince grew sadder and sadder after each place he visited, but he never gave up hope. Then one day, while he was sitting in a tavern on the shores of the Mediterranean Sea, he heard some sailors talk about a mad princess who had come to Greece on a strange wooden horse. The king who had found her, they said, was asking all the doctors in the land to cure her so that he could marry her. He was offering one of his palaces in reward.

For the first time in months, Kamar el Akmar smiled. Within moments he had made a plan to disguise himself as a learned doctor and present himself to the king.

"Who are you and where do you come from?" asked the King of Greece when the prince was brought before him.

"I am a learned Persian doctor and I travel the world curing people," answered Kamar el Akmar. "I have heard of the princess's illness, so I have come to your palace to offer my services."

"She is the most beautiful woman I have ever set eyes on," said the king, "but alas, ever since I decided to marry her she has been most uncontrollable. She came with a strange ebony horse, which I have deposited in my treasury, and an ugly old man whom she said had abducted her — he is in my dungeons. If you can help, I shall be forever in your debt."

"May I have a look at this horse, your majesty?" Kamar el Akmar asked. "It may explain her unfortunate condition."

When the horse was brought from the treasury, Kamar el Akmar discreetly tweaked its ears to check whether the horse was still in working order. "Hum, hum," he said to the king. "In my opinion, the horse and the princess are both under a spell. May I be permitted to see the patient alone?"

When Kamar el Akmar entered the chamber of Shams el Nahar, the princess did not recognize him. So she began to moan and groan and writhe about on her bed. Then Kamar el Akmar whispered his name in her ear. At that, the princess uttered a loud cry as if seized by a fit and fell silent.

"Everyone must now leave the room," cried the so-called doctor. "This young lady needs to be left alone." At this, the maidservants all withdrew in a flutter of slippers and veils.

"My darling, you have been so clever," said Kamar el Akmar when everyone had gone. "Your trick has saved you from getting married to this king."

"How will we get out of here?" asked Shams el Nahar.

"You must pretend that you are getting better," said Kamar el Akmar, "but not fully cured, so that I am still called to see you."

Everyone rejoiced to see the foreign princess looking and feeling so much better.

"I believe, your majesty," said the doctor, "that the princess is possessed by a genie who resides in the wooden horse. The way to cure this affliction is to take them both to the pasture where you first found them so that I can perform a ritual and free them of this evil spirit."

The grateful king arranged for the entire court to watch the proceedings. When they reached the spot where the princess had been found, Kamar el Akmar told the king: "Your majesty, I shall first light a circle of fire around the horse to burn herbs and incense and chase away the evil genie living inside it. Do not be alarmed when you see the horse rocking backwards and forwards, for it will be trying to get rid of the genie."

"Do what needs to be done," answered the king.

"Your majesty," added Kamar el Akmar, "I must also advise you that the princess has to be seated on the horse when I chant my incantations."

"Do your job the best way you can," said the king, "and you will be handsomely rewarded."

"Oh! Just one last thing, your majesty," said Kamar el Akmar. "I too need to be on the horse, in case it throws the princess off its back."

"Yes, yes!" said the king. "Let's get this over and done with."

So Kamar el Akmar sprang on to the horse's back behind Shams el Nahar, rode it into the flames and twisted its right ear. The horse rocked back and forth. The king and his guards could not see what was happening behind the

103

smoke, but suddenly one of them shouted: "Your majesty, look up, look up, the horse is flying away!"

"Come back!" shouted the king. "Guards, draw your bows!"

But it was too late. The ebony horse was already flying through the sky like a great bird, carrying the lovers back to Persia. This time, Kamar el Akmar took no risks; he landed right in front of his father's palace.

The whole city rejoiced at the return of their prince and his beautiful bride. The wedding feast lasted for forty days and forty nights, during which time an envoy was sent to the King of Sanaa informing him of his daughter's safe return and her marriage to the Persian prince. Kamar el Akmar also sent an invitation to his father-in-law, asking him to come and visit, together with a casket full of jewels and gold as a sign of goodwill.

On the final night of the wedding, Shah Sabur slipped away from the festivities and into the stables. And do you know what he did? He broke the levers in the ebony horse's ears to make sure that his son would never be able to ride it again.

The Singing Tree

Once upon a time in the land of Persia there lived a shah called Khusrau. Now, this shah liked to disguise himself as a pauper and wander the streets after dinner, eavesdropping on his subjects. He believed it to be the only way to discover what was going on in his kingdom.

One evening, as Khusrau was passing through a poor district of the city, he heard three sisters having a lively discussion. He stopped outside the closed shutters of a window and listened.

"I wish I was married to the shah's baker," said one voice. "I would have freshly baked bread every morning and invite my friends for tea and cakes every afternoon."

"I wish I was married to the shah's cook," said a second voice. "I would have delicious stews at lunchtime and invite my friends for sumptuous dinners."

"I wish I was married to the shah himself," said another voice, the sweetest of the three. "Then you could both come and live with me in the palace and we would all dress in the nicest clothes and have wonderful parties."

Khusrau smiled indulgently at these words, then headed back to the palace. But that night he could not sleep. He kept on hearing that voice as sweet as a bulbul's saying: "I wish I was married to the shah."

So the next morning, he called his grand vizier and said: "Bring those three sisters to the palace immediately." And he described the exact location of their home. The sisters were in all of a fluster when they arrived. They were even more astounded when the shah said to them: "Do you remember what you were telling each other last night? Well, it is about to come true."

"You," he told the eldest sister, "will marry my chief baker. And you," he told the second sister, "will marry my chief cook. And you, fair one," he told the youngest sister, "you shall marry the shah!"

The wedding festivities happened that same night — two weddings in the servants' quarters and the third one in the great hall. This made the older sisters immensely jealous. From that day on they were determined to destroy their sister's marriage.

The shah was so in love with his young and lovely wife that nothing was good enough for her. He covered her with splendid jewels and silken robes, and he went everywhere with her until she fell pregnant with their first child.

One day while the shah was out hunting, his wife gave birth to a beautiful little boy. Exhausted by the birth, she summoned her older sisters for help. But they did a very evil thing — they took the baby away, wrapped him in a blanket, placed him in a basket and let it float downriver.

When the queen awoke, she found a little puppy sleeping in her bed. "Look at what our queen has given birth to!" said her sisters, pretending to be astonished.

The shah came back to find his wife in tears. "I must have married a djinn," he thought to himself. But he did not dismiss his young wife, as her sisters had hoped. Soon she was heavily pregnant with their second child. This time, she gave birth to another baby boy. Once again, she called on her older sisters for help. And once again, the older sisters took the baby away, wrapped him in a blanket, placed him in a basket and let it float downriver.

When the queen awoke this time, she found a little kitten sleeping next to her in her bed. Khusrau's mood turned dark. "My wife cannot be fully human," he thought. "But what can I do? I love her too much; I must give her one last chance."

And so another year passed and the queen gave birth to a little girl. This time the evil sisters replaced the baby with a small lamb. Like her two brothers before her, the baby was placed in a basket and left to float downriver.

"Enough is enough," said the angry shah. "I am sending my wife to a farm, along with her cat, dog and lamb, for that is exactly where she belongs."

So the poor queen was sent into exile. As for the shah, he was too angry to consider looking for another wife. However, Allah in his infinite mercy had other plans. Each of the children was found by the head gardener, who lived at the far end of the palace grounds. He and his wife were childless, so they were overjoyed at the arrival of three beautiful babies. They called the first boy Fareed, which means "Unique"; the second boy they named Fouad, which means "Heart"; and the baby girl they called Feyrouz, which means "Turquoise."

The head gardener and his wife ensured that the children were brought up well and were given a fine education. When they grew old, the shah, in appreciation of his long and excellent service, gave his former servant a country house with enough land to design his ideal garden. The head gardener turned his plot into a small paradise, with gurgling fountains and exotic plants, shady trees and meandering paths. There the family spent some very precious days together.

But all good things come to an end, and after a few years the head gardener and his wife passed away. The children became even closer now. Fareed and Fouad took great care of Feyrouz, and she made it her task to look after her father's garden the way he would have wanted.

One day, as Fareed and Fouad were out hunting, an old woman stopped by the house asking for shade and water. Touched by her suffering, Feyrouz took her into the house, offered her refreshment and invited her to rest under the boughs of her favorite cedar. When the old woman awoke from her sleep, she thanked Feyrouz and asked her for a tour of the garden. Feyrouz happily obliged, telling her guest all about the plants, the trees, the birds and the fountains. The old woman did not utter a word, just nodding her head in response.

"So, good woman," asked Feyrouz at last, "what do you think of my father's garden?"

The old woman cleared her throat and said: "Well, my dear child, this is indeed one of the most beautiful gardens I have ever seen. However, if I may be frank, there are a few things missing from it."

"Missing!" exclaimed Feyrouz. "What can be missing?"

"Your garden will never be complete without three essential elements, my dear," replied the old woman. "What your garden truly needs is a speaking bird, a singing tree and golden water."

"And how will I find this bird and this tree and this water?" asked Feyrouz.

"Anyone who follows the road from your house and rides for twenty days can find these marvelous items if, on the twentieth day, they ask the first person they meet about them," said the old woman. And with these words, she took her leave of Feyrouz and went on her way.

When Fareed and Fouad returned that evening, Feyrouz was silent and preoccupied, quite unlike her usual talkative self.

"Is something bothering you, dear Feyrouz?" asked her brothers.

"There is," she answered, "but I would feel silly telling you."

They only got the full story after much teasing and cajoling and promising not to laugh at her too much. "I shall go and find the speaking bird and the singing tree for you tomorrow," declared Fareed. "And in case you worry about me, here is my dagger. If any blood appears on it, you will know that I am in grave danger. If not, you may be sure that I am safe."

Feyrouz secured the dagger to her belt in a silver sheath studded with precious stones. At dawn, Fareed saddled his horse and galloped away, only stopping to sleep, eat and pray. On the twentieth day, he came across an old dervish sitting under a shady tree with a large sack beside him.

"Wise man, can you please tell me where I can find the speaking bird, the singing tree and the golden water?" Fareed inquired.

"Are you aware of the dangers you will have to face to obtain these marvelous items?" the dervish asked.

"I will face any difficulty to make my sister Feyrouz happy," replied Fareed.

"Then listen carefully," said the dervish, reaching into his sack and bringing out a round metal bowl. "Take this bowl and throw it in front of you. Let it roll until it stops. Ride your horse to where the bowl lands. Dismount from your horse and leave the bridle over its neck. As you go up the hill, you will see to right and left a great quantity of black stones. Don't stop. You will also hear voices making all kinds of unpleasant comments. Don't look behind or you will instantly be transformed into a black stone. If you reach the top of the mountain without looking back, you will see a cage with the bird you seek."

"What about the singing tree and the golden water?" asked Fareed.

"Ask the speaking bird and he will tell you where to find them," replied the old man.

So Fareed mounted his horse and threw the bowl as far as he could. The bowl rolled for a long time until it stopped at the foot of a mountain scattered with black stones. He dismounted, left the bridle over the horse's neck and began to climb. He had barely walked a few steps when the voices that the old dervish had warned him of began to whisper in his ear: "Where are you going, you fool? What do you want from this mountain?"

Other voices shouted: "Stop thief! Stop! Go back home! There is no speaking bird here!" Other voices shouted: "Kill him, catch him, quarter him!" while others answered: "No, don't touch him, leave him alone, do not hurt him!"

Ignoring all the voices, Fareed climbed up and up until the voices became so strong they gave him a headache. His hands started sweating and his knees trembling.

"What's the matter with me?" he thought. "I am feeling so weak I don't think I can carry on. I'd better turn back." But the moment he turned his head, he was transformed into a black stone. Down at the bottom of the mountain, his horse became a black stone as well.

That evening, Feyrouz pulled the dagger out of its sheath and discovered it was covered in blood. She started sobbing inconsolably. Fouad ran to see what was the matter. At the sight of the bloodied dagger he put his arms around Feyrouz to console her.

"It's my fault," she cried. "I wish I had never listened to that old witch!"

"I know how much you want that bird," said Fouad. "So I shall fetch it for you and find out what has happened to our dear brother as well."

"Please don't go, dear Fouad!" Feyrouz begged. "I could not bear it if anything happened to you as well."

But her brother wouldn't be swayed.

"Take my amber worry beads," said Fouad. "If they run smoothly, I am safe; if they stop moving I am in grave danger."

Feyrouz took the worry beads and wrapped them around her wrist. Then she kissed her brother good-bye and retired to her room to pray for his safe return.

After twenty days of hard riding, Fouad met the same old dervish that Fareed had met. "Peace be with you, wise one," he said. "Can you please tell me where I can find the speaking bird, the singing tree and the golden water?"

"A young man who looked very much like you asked me this question not so long ago," answered the dervish.

"It must have been my brother," said Fouad.

"Poor young man," sighed the dervish. "He must be now one of those numerous stones scattered over that mountain."

"And how does one reach the mountain?" asked Fouad.

"I wish I did not know," said the dervish gloomily. "But the truth has to be told."

He then took a round metal bowl from his sack and gave Fouad exactly the same instructions that he had given Fareed.

Fouad threw the bowl as far as he could. It rolled for a long time and stopped at the foot of the mountain scattered with black stones. There Fouad dismounted, hugged his horse and stood for a while gathering his courage, determined that he would reach the top. He had barely walked a few steps, however, when the voice of a man shouted behind him: "Stop thief, you're trespassing on my mountain!"

Without thinking, Fouad turned his head to speak to the man, but was instantly transformed into a black stone, together with his horse.

Poor Feyrouz! When she ran the amber beads through her fingers that afternoon, they were stiff and heavy. She knew then that Fouad was in grave danger. This time, she did not waste time crying. Instead, she took some of her brother's clothes, disguised herself as a man, jumped on her favorite horse and rode for twenty days to the place where the old dervish lived.

Alighting from her horse, she asked the old man: "Good uncle, have you seen two handsome young men looking for the speaking bird and the singing tree?"

"You must be the exceptional young woman they were trying to please," said the old dervish, smiling. "Nothing can disguise your beautiful voice."

"I beg you, good uncle, to help me find them," pleaded Feyrouz.

"They came to me a while ago and I gave them the same instructions that I will give you," said the old man, reaching into his sack. "Take this bowl and throw it as far as it goes and when it stops, you must stop, leave your horse and climb the mountain. The difficult part is to resist the voices that will shout at you from the mountain."

"How can I resist them?" asked Feyrouz anxiously.

"You must have a quiet mind and the eyes of a falcon fixed on its prey," the dervish answered. "And you must never look behind you or you will be transformed into a black stone."

"I can be like a falcon," said Feyrouz, "I have gone hunting with my brothers many times and have observed these princely birds fixing their prey. But how do I quiet my mind?"

"By ignoring the voices," replied the dervish.

"I have an idea," said Feyrouz. "I will stuff my ears with scraps of cloth."

"Splendid idea," said the dervish, smiling. "Remember the falcon!" he went on. "Focus on your goal and don't look back!"

"Thank you," said Feyrouz, and she threw the bowl in front of her as far as it would roll. "Remember the falcon," she repeated to herself.

Feyrouz then calmly climbed the mountain, looking neither right nor left and not hearing the cacophony of voices. She kept her gaze focused on the mountaintop until she could see the cage with the speaking bird in it. As if from afar, for she still had the pieces of cloth in her ears, she heard the speaking bird say: "Stop — don't move, don't come any closer."

But Feyrouz was determined to get hold of that cage, so she ran the last few yards with her eyes fixed on the bird. "I've got you!" she shouted, grabbing the handle. "Now you're mine!" The moment Feyrouz took hold of the cage, the bird inside it started singing so she took the pieces of cloth out of her ears to hear him. Feyrouz was enchanted, but she knew her work was not yet over. "Tell me where to find the singing tree," she said.

"Turn around and you will see a wood with the singing tree right in the middle of it," said the bird. "You need only take a branch of the tree to plant in your garden."

The moment Feyrouz entered the wood, she saw a

magnificent tree overshadowing the others. "I don't think I have ever heard such a beautiful tune," she thought to herself as she listened to the exquisite tinkling of its leaves. Approaching the tree, she begged its pardon as she carefully broke off one of its lower branches. Returning with the branch to the speaking bird, she said, "Now I need you please to tell me how to find the golden water."

"That's simple," said the bird in his beautiful voice. "If you sit still for a while, you will hear the sound of a gurgling stream. Just follow the sound and you will soon see the golden water."

Following the bird's instructions, Feyrouz found the stream. The golden water was as bright as shooting stars on a summer night. "This is truly one of the most beautiful sights I have ever seen," said Feyrouz to herself as she filled a small flask she had brought with her.

"I have one more task to accomplish," said Feyrouz when she had returned to the singing bird, "and that is to find my brothers."

"Sprinkle a drop of golden water over every black stone you encounter on your way down the hill," the bird advised, "and among them you will find your brothers."

Feyrouz made her way down the hill, sprinkling a drop of golden water on every black stone she passed. Every stone turned into either a human being or a horse. Soon, dozens of young men were stretching their limbs and yawning as if waking from a long sleep, and horses were neighing and shaking their manes and limbs. When Feyrouz finally reached the stones that were her brothers, transforming them with the magic water, all three of them wept tears of joy at being reunited.

The three of them returned home and hung the cage of the speaking bird by a pergola covered with golden and purple grapes. They planted the branch of the singing tree in the middle of the garden, where it took root and grew to become the most beautiful tree of all. They then poured the golden water into one of the fountains where it surged in beautiful glistening jets, splashing and sparkling by day and by night. It looked as if they would all live happily ever after in their beautiful house and garden.

The news of the garden with the speaking bird, the singing tree and the golden water spread far and wide. Many people came to see these wonders with their own eyes. Feyrouz was a graceful, kind and patient hostess, who greatly enjoyed showing her father's garden to her many visitors. Seeing their sister so happily occupied in this way, Fareed and Fouad returned to their favorite pastime: hunting.

One day, as the brothers were riding in pursuit of a fox, they came upon Shah Khusrau's hunting party. "May the blessings of Allah and his Prophet be upon you, your majesty," said the two brothers, dismounting and prostrating themselves before the shah.

"Who are you, young men?" asked Khusrau, strangely stirred by this encounter.

"We are the sons of your late head gardener," replied Fareed, "and it would please us enormously if you were to pay a visit to our father's garden."

"Indeed!" said the shah. "I have heard fascinating stories about your garden. It would please me immensely to see it."

"We could not have wished for a greater honor," said Fouad. "Would your majesty care to honor us with his presence tomorrow?"

When the shah agreed, the brothers rushed to their sister to tell her the good news. "I wish mother was here," said Feyrouz with tears in her eyes. "I have no idea how to entertain a shah."

"Let's ask the speaking bird," suggested Fareed.

"That's an excellent idea," replied Feyrouz, rushing to the garden. "Speaking bird! O speaking bird," she asked, "what does one offer a shah?" And the bird replied:

Shahs like nothing better than eating baked cucumber
Stuffed with fresh pearls on toasted bread and butter.

"You mean stuffed with rice, surely?" said Feyrouz.

"No, I mean pearls," answered the speaking bird.

The following day a big fanfare announced the arrival of the shah. Feyrouz and her brothers rushed to greet him. They led him to the garden and invited him to sit under the pergola while the speaking bird sang a tune of welcome.

After taking some refreshment, the young people showed Khusrau the fountain where the golden water tumbled and splashed. "This is truly a wonderful sight," said the shah. Then, turning to Feyrouz, he asked her to lead him to the singing tree. As she walked ahead, he could not help but admire her graceful demeanor, her elegant dress and her delicate hands. It was a pity he could not see her face for she had covered it with a veil, so that only her eyes were visible.

"How lucky my head gardener was to have such wonderfully handsome and loving children," Khusrau thought to himself. "Why did I have to have such bad luck and be given a cat, a puppy and a lamb instead?" Out loud, he inquired of Feyrouz: "What age are you, my child?"

"Sixteen years old, sire," she replied.

"That's the age my youngest child would have been," thought Khusrau. But his musings were interrupted by a melody so enchanting that he believed Feyrouz and her brothers must have hired an orchestra for his visit and hidden it in the garden. "This is such beautiful music," he said to his young hostess. "I must congratulate the musicians."

"The music is made by the singing tree, sire," explained Feyrouz. "It changes with the time of day and the weather. The tunes become sad when it is cold and happy when it is warm. The tree is quiet during the night and vivacious during the day. No tune is ever the same."

"How lucky you are to have such a garden," replied the shah. "You must count your blessings every day."

"Indeed we do, sire," replied Feyrouz.

"This music and the walk have whetted my appetite," declared the shah. "Let's see if your cook can conjure up a meal as exquisite as the music of this tree!"

The meal was served under the pergola by the cage of the speaking bird. But you should have seen the shah's face when he realized that the cucumbers were stuffed with pearls! "What is this?" he cried angrily. "Are you trying to poison me?"

Before the brothers or their sister could answer, the speaking bird piped up:

Why is it such a surprise to see cucumbers stuffed with pearls? Didn't your majesty surmise when your wife gave birth to animals that she was somewhat diabolical?

"That is what her sisters told me," answered the shah, visibly shaken.

"And why did you believe those old witches?" sang the bird.

"Because I saw the animals with my own eyes," answered the shah.

"The eyes of the heart are the only eyes that truly see," said the bird. Then he added:

> *Look around you and look afresh*
> *At your beautiful sons and daughter,*
> *Blood of your blood and flesh of your flesh.*

Upon hearing these words, Khusrau's heart melted with joy. Was it possible that he was a father after all? When he looked at the smiling faces of Fouad and Fareed, he saw with his heart's eyes and felt deep in his soul that these were truly his children. He stood up to embrace his sons; then he gently lifted the veil from his daughter's face. She looked exactly like her mother!

"I have been such a fool," said the shah, "to have believed those two witches. They have deprived me all these years of the joys of fatherhood." Then, turning to the speaking bird, he asked: "Can you tell us the whole story?"

So the speaking bird told the shah how the head gardener had found the three children as babies, each floating down the stream in a basket; how he had given them the best upbringing and education and taught them how to care for and love each other.

Khusrau rose to embrace his children one more time and told them: "Come, let us mount our horses and ride to the farm where your mother lives. I need to beg for her forgiveness and bring her back to the palace. Then we can be a proper family at long last."

You should have seen the joyful tears that fell from the face of the exiled queen and the kisses she gave to her long-lost children. You should have heard the sighs they all made at the wasted years and the cries of joy that greeted the royal family when they returned to the palace. You should have seen the rice that was thrown over them by the cheering onlookers and the rose petals carpeting the floor. You should have seen the faces of the two evil sisters when they were thrown into the dungeons, kicking and screaming and protesting their innocence.

And you should have seen the magnificent new cage that was made for the speaking bird out of gold filigree studded with precious stones. It hung in the palace courtyard, shaded by trees whose leafy branches attracted all manner of birds, forming an exquisite choir that delighted everyone who heard it.

The Lost Prince

*L*ong ago in a faraway country, lived a king whose son was so perfect and beautiful that he called him Kamar el Zaman, meaning "Time's Moon". The king and his wife couldn't stop looking at him and thanking Allah for their good fortune.

Not only was Kamar el Zaman beautiful but he was studious as well, learning mathematics, history and geography in addition to Arabic and Persian poetry. He was also an accomplished poet himself, a fine calligrapher, and a master chess player. Finally, he was an excellent horseman. When Kamar el Zaman had reached the age of eighteen, the king thought of retiring and handing his son the throne.

"Listen, your majesty," said the grand vizier when the king spoke to him about his plans. "I agree that Kamar el Zaman is destined to be a great king. But it is much better to find him a wife first. A good woman will advise and support him and make him an even better ruler."

"What wise words you speak," said the king. "Let us tell Kamar el Zaman of our decision."

How surprised both men were to see Kamar el Zaman's face darken on hearing what they planned. "I will not even think of marriage before the age of twenty-one," he told his father.

So the king and the grand vizier waited three years before broaching the subject again. But again Prince Kamar el Zaman resisted their proposal: "I'm not interested in marriage!"

"I have been too soft with him," sighed the king. "I have waited three years and he still says no. Guards!" he bellowed. "Take my son to the tower and lock him up for a week with only water and rice to feed him and the Koran for company."

What the king did not know was that the tower was built on the foundations of an old well and that inside the well lived a lady djinn, Maymouna. This djinn was both powerful and beautiful and a creature of the night. The moment the moon rose, she would fly out of the well to meet up with other creatures of the dark.

One evening, as she glided through the night air, Maymouna noticed a light flickering in the tower. Swooping down to investigate, she flew straight in through the window and almost woke Kamar el Zaman from his sleep when she lifted the silken coverlet to take a look at

him. "Praise be to Allah the Creator!" she exclaimed. "I have never seen such a handsome human being in all my life."

Without further thought, Maymouna placed two kisses on Kamar el Zaman's rosy cheeks and another on his forehead, looked at him for a few minutes longer and then flew to meet her friends. She was so taken by the young man that she almost reached the edge of the world without noticing. But she was jolted back to reality when she bumped into one of the ugliest creatures of the dark, a djinn called Dandache, who had huge black wings and dark eyes.

"You wouldn't believe what has just happened to me," said Maymouna.

"And you wouldn't believe what has just happened to me either," replied Dandache. "I have just returned from China, where I have seen the most beautiful princess in the world. Her name is Boudour, and she is indeed as radiant as the moon after which she is named. She has hair as long and lustrous as a horse's tail, eyes as brown as a chestnut and lips as full as a rose in bloom. She is no ordinary princess either – her father loves her so much that he has had seven palaces built specially for her: one for each day of the week."

"Is that all?" asked Maymouna, somewhat annoyed at being so upstaged.

"No, it is not," replied Dandache. "The king is desperate for his daughter to marry so he can have grandchildren but the beautiful princess has refused every suitor who has presented himself, however rich, brave or handsome."

"So what?" replied Maymouna. "Marriage may not be for her."

"That may be the case," answered Dandache. "What is extraordinary is that the princess has saddened her father very much by threatening to kill herself if he presents her with yet another man. So the king has had her locked away in one of her seven palaces, guarded night and day by her old nurse. I live near this palace," Dandache went on, "and every night when the princess is fast asleep, I fly through her window and kiss her on both cheeks."

"This is an amazing story," conceded Maymouna, "because it is the very mirror of mine. I have just met the most handsome prince I have ever seen. He too has been locked away by his father and is sleeping soundly as we speak."

"I bet you that my princess is more beautiful than your prince," taunted Dandache.

"You don't know what you are talking about!" snorted Maymouna.

"Then bring him to China so we can compare the two," suggested Dandache.

"No, you bring her here!" insisted Maymouna.

As the more powerful of the two djinns, in the end she had her way. Dandache spread his huge black wings and flew straight back to China to bring his princess to the tower where Kamar el Zaman slept so peacefully.

Dandache gently deposited the princess next to the prince and both djinns gazed at the two mortals for a while in silence, quite unable to decide who was the more beautiful of the two. Then Maymouna had an idea: "Let's wake them up and see which one expresses greater admiration for the other," she said.

"Perfect," agreed Dandache.

So Maymouna transformed herself into a flea and nibbled Kamar el Zaman on the neck. He woke up with a cry, swatting his neck and looking around to catch the culprit. The first thing he saw was the Chinese princess.

"I must be dreaming," he thought, rubbing his eyes. "Who is this divine creature lying by my side?" He took her hand and tried to rouse her, but Dandache had placed a spell on the princess and she did not stir. "Maybe this is the young woman my father had in mind for a bride," thought the prince. "Maybe that's why he was so upset when I kept refusing to get married. Now I understand why he was so angry."

Then, lifting the princess's hand, he saw that she was wearing an exquisite ring of golden filigree. "Let me put her ring on my finger so that I can show both her and my father the seriousness of my intentions," for he had fallen instantly in love with her.

Then, suddenly overwhelmed with sleep, he lay back in his bed and dozed off. It was now Dandache's turn. He transformed himself into a gnat and bit the princess on her big toe. "Ouch!" she cried. "What was that?"

Of course, she too was startled to find herself not alone but lying beside the most handsome young man she had ever seen. Then she noticed her ring on his little finger. "How did that get there?" she wondered. She took the stranger's hand and shook it hard, but Maymouna's spell was so strong that the sleeping man did not so much as blink!

"Oh well," she sighed. "Maybe he will be awake in the morning and then I can ask him why my ring is on his finger!" Then, feeling suddenly weary, she too drifted back to sleep.

"Now," said Maymouna to Dandache, "which is more handsome? My prince or your princess?"

Dandache had to concede that Kamar el Zaman's beauty was difficult to beat, so he offered to take the princess back to her palace.

In the morning, the first thing Kamar el Zaman did upon waking was to look for the beautiful young woman he had seen beside him during the night. "She cannot have disappeared!" he cried. "I hope this is not yet another of my father's tricks." He called the guard outside the door and asked him: "Where is the beautiful lady who was in my room last night?"

"Our prince is starting to hallucinate all alone in this tower," said the guard to himself. Out loud, he answered the prince politely: "Lady? What lady? There was no lady, beautiful or otherwise, in your room last night, your highness, or I would have noticed."

"You haven't noticed a thing!" said the prince, getting angry. "There was a lady in my room last night. Indeed, I have her ring to prove it!"

The guard did not know how to answer the prince, so he rushed to the king to tell him that his son was having hallucinations and that he should be taken out of the tower at once. The king sent the grand vizier to the tower immediately in order to question his son. Upon hearing about the lady, the vizier said: "How could she have entered your room, your highness, without disturbing the guard?"

"If she wasn't here, where did I get this ring from?" answered Kamar el Zaman angrily. "Go and tell my father that she was indeed here last night and that she is the only one I will ever marry!"

So the grand vizier rushed back to the king but with more questions than answers. This time the king himself came to the tower.

141

"I assure you, father, that there was a beautiful lady sleeping in my chamber last night and this ring is my proof. I beg you to find her because she is the only one I will ever marry!" And with these words the prince took to his bed, refusing all food.

The king was beside himself with worry and called his council to discuss the matter.

In the meantime, far away in the land of China, Princess Boudour woke up to find herself back in her room. "Nurse!" she called. "Where is the young man I saw last night?"

"Young man? What young man, my dear?" answered the old woman, pressing her hand on the princess's forehead to check whether the girl was feverish.

"The young man who took my ring," answered the princess.

"But, my dear child, we left you alone last night. No one could have entered your room!" said the nurse.

"I tell you that my ring has disappeared. See!" she said, showing her bare fingers.

"I'm calling your mother," answered the nurse, who was now quite agitated.

"Darling," said the queen, "you must have misplaced your ring. Besides, no young man would dare enter your private quarters without permission."

"Mother, if you don't believe me I will stay in bed and refuse all food until you find the young man in question, because he is the one I wish to marry!"

So the queen went to her husband. The emperor called his councilors and said: "Announce to everyone that whoever cures my daughter will be given her hand in marriage."

Doctors, magicians, astrologers and wise men of every kind were called to the princess's bedside, but no one could find a cure.

Now, the princess's nurse had a son called Marzavan. He was the same age as Boudour and was like a brother to her as they had grown up together in the palace. He had spent the last few years traveling to many countries in order to sit at the feet of famous sages, and he had just returned to China. On hearing that Boudour was unwell, he rushed to her bedside. She opened her heart to him at once and told him her strange story.

"I believe you, sister," he said. "And I am going to find this young man and bring him to you."

Marzavan traveled for many months until he reached the country where Kamar el Zaman lived. Here, he heard the story of the young prince pining for a young woman he had once seen in a dream.

"This sounds promising!" he thought to himself. And he went immediately to the capital city and asked for an audience. By now, the king was prepared to try anything, so he took his exotic visitor straight to his son's sleeping quarters. Marzavan looked at the prince lying on his bed, eyes half closed, then whispered in his ear: "I know the lady you are looking for. She is Princess Boudour, daughter of Gaiour, Emperor of China, and she has sent me to you."

Kamar el Zaman's eyes flew open.

"Describe this princess to me," he said.

So Marzavan told the prince about Princess Boudour — radiant as the moon, with hair as long and lustrous as a horse's tail, eyes as brown as a chestnut and lips as full as a rose in bloom.

"It's her! It's her!" cried Kamar el Zaman. "Bring me some chicken soup and bread," he commanded his servants. "I am absolutely starving!"

"You must regain your strength fast," said Marzavan.

"Why?" asked Kamar el Zaman between small mouthfuls.

"Because I promised to take you to her," Marzavan replied.

A week later, Kamar el Zaman told his father that he was going hunting with his new friend. "We shall be gone for a few days," he told the king, "so that I can show him the region."

So Kamar el Zaman and Marzavan took two horses each, one for riding and the other for carrying provisions, as well as two grooms to tend the horses. They set off early in the morning and rode all day. When evening came, they stopped at a caravansary for food and rest. While the grooms were asleep, Marzavan asked Kamar el Zaman to give him one of his shirts, offering one of his own in return. Then he went to the stables and brought out three of the four horses.

"Let's go now," whispered Marzavan. "But very quietly, so as not to wake anyone."

The young men rode all night, with one horse in tow, until they reached a forest.

"Do not judge me badly for what I am about to do," said Marzavan to Kamar el Zaman. With these words, he drew his sword and killed the spare horse.

"Why have you killed the horse?" cried Kamar el Zaman. "What has it done to deserve this terrible fate?"

"I had to, my lord," said Marzavan. Then he took the shirt Kamar el Zaman had given him earlier, tore it up and dipped it in the horse's blood, leaving it lying on the ground.

"What are you doing now?" cried Kamar el Zaman in alarm.

"We need to mislead your father's men about your whereabouts. You see, when the grooms wake up and discover that we have gone, they will raise the alarm. Your father will send his troops to look for you. When they find the dead horse and the torn shirt, they will believe you have been killed by bandits and stop looking for you."

"This is a cruel trick to play on an old man," protested Kamar el Zaman.

"I know it is," said Marzavan. "But this is the only way you can travel freely to see your beloved Princess Boudour."

So the young men mounted their horses and left the forest, traveling across mountains, steppes and plains, until they reached China. "Let us stop at an inn for a day or so," said Marzavan. "We need to find you an astrologer's robe."

"You never cease to amaze me!" exclaimed Kamar el Zaman. "Why do I need such a thing?"

"The only way you can enter the king's palace is to pretend to be an astrologer," replied Marzavan. "For Emperor Gaiour has called upon every wise man in this land and beyond to see if he can find a cure for his beloved daughter. Are you ready to act like one?"

"I'll do anything for the princess," said Kamar el Zaman.

"In that case, listen to me," Marzavan went on. "When you reach the palace gates, you will claim to be a famous astrologer from Arabia. In the meantime, I will go into the palace and give my mother a note to take to Princess Boudour."

When the astrologer's robe had been purchased, Kamar el Zaman made his way to the palace. "I am the astrologer of astrologers," he declared, "and I have come all the way from Arabia to cure your beloved princess!"

"Another body for the dungeons," thought the palace guards.

"So, young man," asked the emperor when Kamar el Zaman was brought before him, "I hear you have a cure for my daughter."

"I believe I do, your majesty," replied the prince.

"I cannot believe that such a young man would have the experience needed to cure my beloved daughter," said the king, looking sceptical.

"Put me to the test," answered Kamar el Zaman. "All I need is a quill, ink and paper."

A portable scribe's desk was brought in and Kamar el Zaman sat down, picked up the quill and wrote in his best calligraphic script:

My darling,

Why did you abandon me that night? I have been unable to sleep, eat or enjoy life since you left. Night and day, I think only of you. As a token of my sincere intentions, I return the ring that I took from you that night. This note is not a trick, nor a figment of your imagination. I cannot wait to hold you in my arms at last.

Your loving, pining, desperate

Prince Kamar el Zaman

Folding the paper, he slipped the ring inside, sealed the letter and gave it to the palace guard.

The princess, who had already been warned by Marzavan about Kamar el Zaman's presence in the city, tore open the letter. She did not even read the note as she immediately recognized her ring. "Bring this astrologer to my quarters at once!" she told her nurse. "I already feel so much better!"

The nurse hurried back to the guard, the guard hurried to the king, and the king hastened to his daughter so that he could see her for himself. "The guard did not lie; it is a long time since I've seen those pearly white teeth," said the emperor, embracing his darling daughter with delight.

"Where is the astrologer?" asked Boudour eagerly.

"He is waiting outside your chambers," replied the emperor. "I suspect the young man is more than an astrologer — he is clearly a magician of the heart as well."

"Take me to him, father," said the princess.

Kamar el Zaman stood transfixed at the sight of his beloved Boudour. "She is worth every mile I have traveled," he thought as he approached her. Then, kneeling in front of her, he said: "Here I am at your feet at last."

The princess smiled as she extended her hand and helped him up, saying to her father: "Here is the man who has stolen my heart!"

The emperor laughed, looked at the young couple and said: "I think it is time I heard your story, young man. Let us sit down with a refreshing cup of jasmine tea while you tell me everything."

The Celebrations

When Shahrazade had finished her last story, she said: "Sire, we have sat together for one thousand and one nights, during which you have heard strange and magical tales and traveled to different worlds. I hope that I have distracted you from your anger and soothed your pain, making you think better of women. Can I now ask for a favor?"

"Why now?" asked Shahriyar.

"I have shared with you the jewels of my imagination and the essence of my wisdom and I have nothing more to give," answered Shahrazade. "However, I have one more thing to show you."

"What is it?" said Shahriyar, intrigued.

"Please wait a moment," she whispered, leaving the shah's chamber.

A few minutes later, she returned with three little boys, each as beautiful as the morning star: a baby in her arms, a one-year-old crawling on all fours and a two-year-old clinging to her robe.

"These are your children, whom you have never asked to

see but who wish to meet you," she said, bowing to Shahriyar. With this, she placed the baby in his father's arms, while the other two buried their golden-brown heads in her skirts.

"Come on, children, don't be shy," she said. "Say good morning to your father."

There were a few seconds of silence in which neither the boys nor Shahriyar could speak. Then the baby started crying and Shahriyar did not know what to do, so he handed him clumsily back to his mother.

The other two boys lifted their heads from their mother's robe and looked at their father whose heart leaped with joy at the sight of such beautiful children. Then the elder one said good morning, while the younger smiled like a new moon and babbled in some strange language of his own.

"May I beg you, sire, to think again before killing the mother of your children?" said Shahrazade.

Shahriyar was silent for a few minutes, then he stood up, embraced his wife and said: "For one thousand and one nights you have kept me company, entertained and amused me, relieved me of my boredom and soothed my pain and anger. But, more importantly, with your steadfast love you have made me change my mind about the faithlessness of women. You have become as necessary to me as water is to a garden and as a compass is to a sailor."

Shahrazade hugged her husband with her free arm, the two older boys still clinging to her skirts, and said: "All I ask from you, sire, is to love them as much as you love yourself."

"Or as much as I love you, my dear," said Shahriyar, picking up the one-year-old and bouncing him in the air.

"Me too, father!" cried the two-year-old.

As he picked up his eldest son, Shahriyar turned to his wife and said: "Allah bless you, my dear, and bless your father and your family and the children you gave me. You are a most perfect wife, intelligent and learned, patient and wise. Your place is beside me on this throne and in my heart."

Then, turning to a servant, he said: "Please call the vizier and ask him to come here immediately."

"Vizier," he said, embracing his father-in-law when he appeared, "please meet your grandchildren." The grandchildren, who knew their grandfather well, ran to him with cries of joy while Shahriyar put his arms around Shahrazade, then ordered: "Send after my brother, Shahzaman, ruler of Samarkand, so he can meet my family."

Then Shahriyar declared seven days and seven nights

of celebrations. He ordered Ctesiphon to be decorated with royal banners and tents put up in the palace gardens, all laid out with the most delicious foods — roast lamb, saffron rice, nuts and sweetmeats of every kind. He sent the crier to the market to call on his subjects to come to the palace to eat, drink and celebrate. It was his way of asking for their forgiveness after the years of terror.

So rich and poor, great and small, all came to their shah, congratulating him on his family and good fortune and rejoicing that the dark times were finally over. They ate and drank for seven days and nights and blessed their ruler and his wise and beautiful wife.

The people of Samarkand secretly wished that Shahzaman would also find a good wife like his brother Shahriyar. Some whispered that maybe he should think of marrying Duniazad, Shahrazade's younger sister. But this story we must leave to another time and another book, another day and another night.

Glossary

bulbul A songbird mentioned in medieval Persian poetry; it means "nightingale" in Arabic.

caravan A group of travelers crossing the desert, often traders with several camels, and sometimes horses, to carry their goods.

Ctesiphon One of the great cities of the Persian empire. Located on the east bank of the River Tigris, its ruins are in Iraq, approximately 35 kilometres south of Baghdad.

dervish A member of a religious order, vowed to poverty.

dinar A gold coin, first issued in the seventh century AD. Dinars and dirhams are still the currency in parts of the Middle East, although they are no longer gold and silver!

dirham A silver coin, worth about a twentieth of a dinar.

djinn A spirit able to take on different forms, human and animal. Some djinns are good and some evil.

hammam A steam bath, often referred to as a "Turkish bath." Hammams have been an important part of Middle Eastern culture since ancient times. They are communal baths used for cleansing the body, relaxing and meeting people.

jellabiya A traditional Arab garment.

kohl Black powder traditionally used as eye makeup in the

Middle East. It was originally used as protection against eye ailments and to provide relief from the glare of the sun.

majlis An Arabic term meaning "a place of sitting" and applied to an assembly or parliament.

Persia The historical name of modern-day Iran, but originally applying to a much larger area that would have included what is now Iran, Afghanistan and Pakistan. Founded in 550 BC, it was once a major empire or series of empires ruled by different dynasties.

Samarkand Situated in what is now Uzbekistan, Samarkand is one of the oldest inhabited cities in the world and celebrated for being at the midpoint along the Silk Road, the great trading route between China and the West.

shah A short form of "shahanshah", meaning "king of kings" and equivalent in status to "emperor."

Shahrazade This has been variously spelled in different versions of *The Arabian Nights* ("Scheherazade" is probably the most well-known form of the name) and can mean either "lion-born," "city-freer" or "she whose realm or dominion is noble."

Shahriyar This means "king" or "sovereign" in Persian.

sheikh The leader of a tribe or a man respected for his wisdom or religious knowledge.

souk A Middle Eastern bazaar or market, usually occupying a wide area of twisting narrow streets and therefore very easy for a visitor to get lost in.

vizier A chief councillor (from the Arabic "wazir").

$\mathcal{S}$ources

The author is grateful for the following sources, which she referred to while writing this book:

Burton, Sir Richard E., trans., *The Book of The Thousand Nights and a Night*. USA: Privately printed by The Burton club, 1970.

Haddawy, Husain, trans., *The Arabian Nights*. New York: W. W. Norton & Company, 1990.

Khawam, Rene R., trans., *Les Mille et Une Nuits*. Paris: Phebus Libretto, 1986.

Mahdi, Muhsin, ed. *The Thousand and One Nights*. Leiden: Brill, 1984.